The Dimetrodons, the Dorians, and the Modern World, Synapsid Critical Edition

The Dimetrodons, the Dorians, and the Modern World, Synapsid Critical Edition

Maurice James Blair

Synapsid Revelations Press Corporation

THE DIMETRODONS, THE DORIANS, AND THE MODERN WORLD

ISBN: 978-1-963470-14-7

Blair, Maurice James, 1976-
The Dimetrodons, the Dorians, and the Modern World, Synapsid Critical Edition

Synapsid Revelations Press Corporation
9619 Meadowcroft Dr
Houston, TX 77063
U.S.A.

This work takes the author's self-published 2022 work as a starting point and adjusts it. An outline of the changes: the cleaning up of typographic anomalies that had been present in the fiction; a few other tweaks to portions of the fiction; the removal of, revision to, and addition of select portions of supplemental nonfiction; line-break, indention, alignment Δs, etc. –Synapsid Revelations Press Corporation and Maurice James Blair

References in the nonfiction preliminaries, the between-chapters-two-and-three nonfiction intermediate section, and the nonfiction epilogue and subsequent sections to any businesses, organizations, and individuals do not necessarily mean that there is any endorsement from or other business relationship with any of them.

Publication Date: September 26, 2024

TO WHOM IT MAY CONCERN:

On a scale of risk and reward, running from absolute-zero to infinity-factorial, this book is in the vicinity of the peak of that scale, either arriving at ∞! or approaching it.

The door is open, and you can step through to the other side or you can flee.

Fate and Karma and Opportunity beseech thee, "What shall it be?!"

SELECT COMBAT COORDINATION DIAGRAMS:

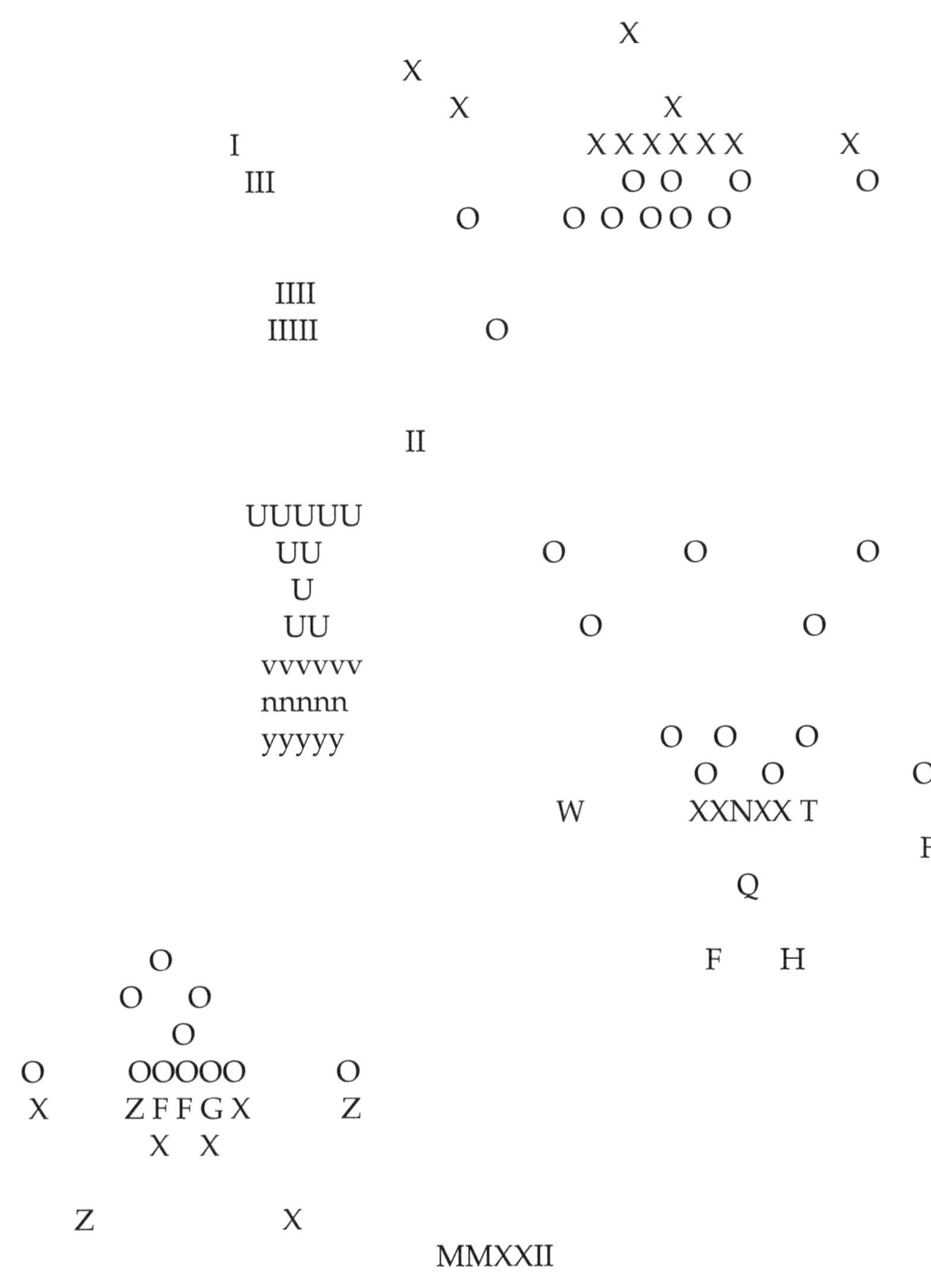

MMXXII

ii

IIIMMXXV

CXXCDEFGHIJ   ZYXWVUTSR

GVGVGVGVGVVVGVVGVAAGVAAAVGGVVGAA

PREFACE

Part One: A transcription of September 3, 2019 correspondence with Dr. Dorsey Armstrong:

My initial inquiry of that day:

Dorrie,

As a reminder, I took your UWC course at Duke in Fall Semester 1994, then I contacted you a few times in the range of 9-10 years ago via e-mail, and you briefly answered via e-mail.

When convenient, please share a few comments about The Dorian Invasion.

If you would prefer to decline comment by not sending a response, then I will interpret that as an alternate expression of emptiness.

If you would prefer to forward this to another, more appropriate member of the Purdue faculty, then please feel free to forward this.

Thank you,

Maurice James Blair
Houston, Texas

Her response, other than a few additional lines that were below her name as part of stating her position within the Purdue University faculty and related activities:

HI Maurice---

Good to hear from you! Alas, I don't actually know thing ONE about the Dorian invasion--in fact I'd never heard of it until your email--so I fear I am out of my depth on this one. Sorry!

Dorsey Armstrong

Here is how I responded a few hours later on that day, September 3, 2019:

Dorrie,

That is fine, very few do. Yet, there is a degree of shared ancestral memory across humankind of the energy emanating from the ancient legend of when The Dorians annihilated The Mycenaen culture.

On a related note, at about 5:52 PM CDT today, Tuesday, September 3rd, 2019, I entered a Google search for "dorian and mycenaen teamwork" and it gave a result of not matching any documents. I have attached the related pdf.

No need to apologize. You have provided useful information.

...

Recently, I again listened to "Kashmir" by Led Zeppelin. Soon after sending this message
I will again listen to "Man on the Moon" by R.E.M.

I listened to slightly more than half of Sgt. Pepper [by The Beatles] a while earlier today, yet the CD playback method appeared to encounter a magnetic anomaly early into the 8th track, and I jumped over to listening to portions of Houses of the Holy [by Led Zeppelin].

Regards,

Maurice James Blair

A September 20, 2024 comment on that earlier correspondence: I intentionally used the word "when" rather than the word "how" in the phrase "when The Dorians" because I believed myself to already as of September 3, 2019 known a huge percentage of the "how" yet intending to tune in better with the timeliness of how those who should become the instruments of righteously-indignant, divine wrath can choose the correct timing of when to do that. Consider exploring *The Science, Religion, Politics, and Cards Trilogy*, which consists of *Science, Religion, Politics, and Cards* (2023), *Alternative Beginnings and Endings of All Things* (2024), and *Simplicity, Intricacy, and Beyond* (2024) to better understand the context of this.

Here is a copy of the September 3, 2019 Google Search, converted to black-and-white-and-gray:

Here is a zoomed-in & rearranged view of that:

"dorian and mycenaen teamwork"

All Images Videos News

Your search - **"dorian and mycenaen teamwork"** - did not match any documents.

Suggestions:

- Make sure all words are spelled correctly.
- Try different keywords.
- Try more general keywords.

9/3/2019

Google

"dorian and mycenaen teamwork" - Google Search

Shopping More Settings Tools

77063, Houston, TX - From your device - Use precise location - Learn more

Help Send feedback Privacy Terms

/search?ei=ue5uXdjqDIn0tAXO9q_gAg&q="dorian+and+mycenaen+teamwork"&oq="dorian+and+mycenaen+teamwork"&gs_l...

Part Two: Here is a nonfiction narrative that I composed on September 16, 2024, then lightly edited on September 25, 2024:

"An Tale of A Canine and Several Humans, or: A Nonfiction Mostly-Circa-1982 Story Presented in Third-Person Omniscient Voice"

by Maurice James Blair

The extraordinarily tough male canine that went by the name Toughy and served both as a pet and as a guard dog at the ranch that Maurice A.T. Blair owned (and at which he permitted his uncle and aunt to work) loomed as a threat to multiple people.

M.A.T. Blair normally pronounced his "Maurice" name in reference to himself like many normally pronounce "Morris" yet often went by the name "Ted," which reduced confusion since his uncle Maurice T. Hoppe went by "Maurice" with the "Morris" pronunciation. There was a rather storied history of what happened between that canine and many of the humans with whom it interacted.

Toughy was a mixed breed dog of Collie, German Shepherd, and Australian Dingo heritage, and he had no fear of human beings. Well, there were in some ways two exceptions to that: Toughy had fierce loyalty to and therefore at least a microscopic edge of fear toward, at first, one human master, and, later, two human masters: at first, only Maurice T. Hoppe, later, adding Ted Blair.

One of the things that many people in Park County, Montana were aware of was that when they would visit that ranch, each time they dared to step onto the property, Toughy just might run over and grasp one of their Achilles tendons with some light-to-medium pressure. In many such cases, Toughy would use his teeth to hold steady until commanded by either M.T.H. or M.A.T.B. to let go. You see, although none of the humans had made an attempt to train the dog to do that, it had taken its own initiative to use that method as a way of territoriality.

Things had changed, though. Ted married a woman in 1975, and his wife gave birth to a child the next year. Yes, Ted continued owning the ranch, yet, as it had been for many years, he would go for great stretches of time between stays there. After suddenly retiring from defense contracting due to health concerns while the wife and son were on a vacation overseas to be with extended relatives, he moved from New Hampshire back to Montana. His wife and son had been on an extended vacation overseas, in connection with one of his sisters-in-law having an extravagant wedding. That wedding went well, adding a brother-in-law to Ted's list of extended relatives. Ted retired from Raytheon while his wife and son were on vacation, and he had then moved from the Northeastern U.S. back to Montana.

Ted Blair knew that his wife and their five-year-old child would be departing Taiwan to go to Montana and join him on the ranch.

He also knew Toughy through and through.

March 1982 was rapidly approaching, and that would be when his wife and son would join him, his uncle, and his aunt as residents of the ranch. The situation begged the question, "What should happen next with Toughy?"
Ted considered options.

What if he were to try to sell Toughy? That seemed a recipe for disaster, as Toughy could likely wind up killing the new owner if deeming him or her to not be acting right or if simply not warming up enough to the new would-be master.

What if he were to simply keep Toughy around? That also seemed problematic, as he could not bear to leave his wife and young child vulnerable to getting maimed or killed by Toughy.

What about taking Toughy to a veterinarian to be euthanized? Ted decided against that as well; he believed there might be a sizable risk that the veterinarian would unsuspectingly treat Toughy like a normal dog and at some stage fail to take enough precautions, resulting in Toughy doing the unthinkable, turning the tables by euthanizing the veterinarian instead of the other way around.

Ted took Toughy out away from where his uncle and aunt or anyone else might be able to see what would be happening.

Somewhere on that ranch, he ordered, "Toughy, here!" As he did that, he pointed to a spot where he intended for Toughy to place his nose.

Toughy obediently placed his nose to that spot.

Ted then shot Toughy through the brain, euthanizing the canine then and there.

After that, Ted buried Toughy somewhere out there, returned to the ranch, and withheld from his Uncle Maurice Hoppe that he--Ted Blair--had executed one of the beloved family pets because he found it to be the best choice in the situation.

The son of Maurice A.T. Blair would not find out about this story until years later. The father waited until he believed it the right time to let his son know about how that situation had unfolded.

On a lighter note, early in life that son often went by "Jimmy" in connection with his middle name "James." Later, he shifted over to mainly going by "Jim." After that, at some stage he became aware of the powerful presence in the sitcom *Bewitched* (1964-1972) of the character "Maurice" going by the main conventional American English way of pronouncing "Maurice," and he decided for a while to go over to primarily going by that as his main spoken individual name. Several times over the years, Maurice A.T. Blair whereas the father would mention to his son, his only known child, that he noticed that the son would most often pronounce that shared individual name in a different way for himself the son than the father would most often pronounce that name for himself the father.

On a heavier note, as a teenager, during some phase, Maurice J. Blair read from beginning to end the novella *Of Mice and Men*. That reading happened circa 1992.

Eventually, that M.J.B. fellow grew to become an adult man.

In the long run his memories of that 1937 literary work that was brilliantly written by John Steinbeck (1902-1968), the tale of the canine Toughy, and many strange personal experiences served to afford extra depth perception of realities beyond the veneers of societies.

*   *   * * * * * * * * ** *** ***** *********** *********** ***** **** ** * * * * * * * *   *   *

Part Three of the Preface: Supplements to Parts One and Two

••• Part One included transcription of an email that had declined to italicize *Sgt. Pepper* (1967) and *Houses of the Holy* (1973).

••• Adjacent to Part Two were some conversations in which Ted spoke about things that involved: (a) wartime catastrophic damage to the genitals of people of diverse demographics (male, female, young, old, etc.) and (b) how among some of his associates of way back when—whether during combat or away from combat— there were conversations that referred to human flesh as tasting similar to pork yet sweeter, and, therefore, nicknamed "sweet pig."

Here is a bibliography of several news stories that may serve as additional warm up with which to gear up for the intensity of this novella's story telling:

• amNY. "The Case of 'The Butcher of Tompkins Square Park'." (02 FEB 2012).
   https://amny.com/news/the-case-of-the-butcher-of-tompkins-square-park (as accessed on 18 JUL 2024).

• Rowman & Littlefield International. "Wartime Sexual Violence Against Men: The Hidden Face of Warfare." (28 NOV 2018). Colloquium. Republished by Medium.   https://medium.com/colloquium/warfare-sexual-violence-against-men-21ae5b15b3c (as accessed on 04 JUN 2024).

• Waterman, Cole. "Man accused of torturing woman, hiding body in Saginaw Township motel wants to know how she died." (24 SEP 2024). MLive.
   https://www.mlive.com/news/saginaw-bay-city/2024/09/man-accused-of-torturing-woman-hiding-body-in-saginaw-township-motel-wants-to-know-how-she-died.html (as accessed on 24 SEP 2024)

* *

THE DIMETRODONS, THE DORIANS, AND THE MODERN WORLD,
SYNAPSID CRITICAL EDITION

PREFACE, CONTINUED

PART FOUR: A MOVIE LIST SURVIVAL GUIDE BOTH FOR HOW TO SURVIVE
ENCOUNTERING THIS BOOK AND, TO SOME DEGREE, HOW TO SURVIVE
THE SLINGS AND ARROWS OF OUTRAGEOUS FORTUNE IN GENERAL

• If you believe yourself to have a main problem involving romantic love, sex, and courtship, then some movies to perhaps compare and contrast with your situation are *500 Days of Summer* (2009), *Ghost* (1990), *The Groundstar Conspiracy* (1972), *The Valachi Papers* (1972), *Two Girls and a Guy* (1997), and *Bruce Almighty* (2003).

• If you currently revolve the most around money, career, and finances, then perchance it would prove productive to consider *Barbarians at the Gate* (1993), *The Disappearance of Aimee* (1976), and *The Firm* (1993).

• If you are most concerned with freedom, responsibility, subjugation, liberty, and ethics, then consider exploring *Spartacus* (1960), *Abraham Lincoln vs. Zombies* (2012), *Casino* (1995), *Everest* (1998), and *Transformers One* (2024).

PREAMBLE:

Special thanks to The Ancient Beings of Yester-Centuries,
Yester-Millennia, *and Bygone Eras Further Back Than That.*

Dedication to The Beings of the Modern World,
The Beings of the Future,
and The Beings of The Utterly Beyond.

CONTENTS

INTRODUCTION

Think back to the earliest strongly vivid memory you have of a conversation that affected you by presenting an extremely taboo reference. Something that somehow registered into your mind, whether or not you immediately recognized it for what it was. Many probably partially registered such an occurrence when very young.

Perhaps in your case it is something that you would seldom, if ever, dare to speak about in public, yet which you might remember vividly.

For some it might have been an NC-17-type of extreme S&M torture reference in seventh grade, for others it might have been a conversation that they witnessed on either the silver screen or TV. Thinking more broadly, there are many taboo and generally uncomfortable topics and scenarios, and it varies very much from one person to another the interest in this or that, the repulsion toward this or that, etc. Although this work does not primarily dwell on such stuff, it does every so often delve into extreme violence, bizarre sexual situations, the occult, wild parties, etc. Imagine, if you will, your life in relation to world history, including normal competition, deviant competition, negotiations, teamwork, illusions, and truth.

Very relevant could be the article, "Life Finds a Way" by Doyle Irvin. (American Forests, 2017; Cf. https://www.americanforests.org/article/life-finds-a-way/ as accessed on August 5, 2023). If one embraces the broadest perspectives about roles in the creation of projects, then one might think, *If we were alive before the finalization of any given literary work, then we were to some degree—however infinitesimal or however integral—part of THE TEAM OF THE PROCESSES OF REALITY that together led to the development of that work, by our mere presence in reality prior to the completion of that development.*

There are many different ways that sentient beings could debate this, some taking positions against it, others taking positions for it.

It seems likely that among those opting to debate this, a high percentage of the pro-mystically-inclined would choose to side with favoring that proposition, whereas a high percentage of the anti-mystically-inclined would choose to side with opposing that proposition. The fiction of this novella includes portrayals of beings who embrace pro-mysticism, anti-mysticism, male power, female power, freedom of speech, holy war, holy peace, the full range of politics, etc.

This text could prove helpful to explorers of political science, comparative religion, psychology, Dharma talks, management science, Sunday School classes, Thursday School classes, Wednesday School classes, sex education, gender studies, business, and geopolitical events. History, absurdism, science fiction, fantasy, practicality, realism, horror, and paradox abound.

–M.J.B., September 20-26, 2024

Chapter One: 11G Wireless

It was a cocktail party for paleontologists, and it occurred at a Hilton hotel in Houston, TX. The vast majority of the attendees were men, only a few spouses were present, and a few single females and males of neither the categories of paleontologist nor spouse-of-paleontologist were there, including five groupies, six paid escorts, and two news reporters. The atmosphere was festive. 27% of the attendees had been listening to the classic rock radio station KKRW 93.7 FM "The Arrow."

A rather quiet-at-times and talkative-at-times bloke of the name Charlie Jacob Soros chose to remain very silent and observant for this gathering from its outset. He had listened to the aforementioned frequency modulation radio channel on his drive to the gathering, which started at 7:30 PM. Jacob arrived at 7:37 PM. By 9:45 PM he sensed that he just might spring into action if everything would align to make it the right time. He looked at his watch and subvocalized in his mind's auditorium, "9:47 PM, 9th of October, 1999."

He stood in the corner, silent and ready. Nearby, he overheard two men who were mildly under the influence of vodka and other beverages. They were discussing their wives, both of whom were conveniently absent.

"Thank God she isn't here right now," said Charlie G. Watts. "Although I love her - most of the time, anyway, mind you - I've got the feeling that if she was here right at this time, she'd be fucking up my ability to get half or more of our conversations to go pretty much the way I like them. If you don't mind my asking, how do you feel right now about how Cheryl isn't here?"

Sammy answered, "Well, it's a mixed blessing, which might also be to say it's a mixed curse." Both men had wives named Cheryl, yet C.G.W.'s usually went by the name Shirley.

"How so?" inquired Charlie.

Sammy said, "Well, you know. I love her deeply quite often, and, of course, sometimes there's that explosive mixture of love and hate. Then there are those times when she and I are maybe on the brink of pulling out a pistol or a machete and acting out bloody murder!"

Charlie G.W. thought for a few seconds, then stated gently, "Yes, I do kind of know what you mean. My old man used to say that love and hate go hand and glove, only you don't always know which is the hand and which is the glove."

Sammy whispered something inaudible to Charlie, then said in a very audible voice, "Love and hate *are often not together*! Just because someone loves or hates someone at a given time, it doesn't mean they both love and hate them then and there! *Sometimes it does, sometimes it doesn't!* Oh, yes, there are so many philo-sophical debates, and all the classic religious ideas, but I can *feel* it within me, *often* you *can* have the one without the other!"

"Cool it, calm down, easy tiger," said the Watts fellow with the name Charlie.

Sammy continued, "Well, maybe a better way to look at this would be some parallel to tennis or football. Shit happens, people have goals, their goals don't always match, more stuff happens. And so on and so on. It's convenient that we have words for our emotions, but maybe there are primary drivers that are more fundamental than them."

The other Charlie in the vicinity, Charlie J. Soros, had heard what Sammy Watts had whispered to his distant relative C.G. Watts just a little while earlier, and it had been, "Son of a gun." That C.J.S. often went by the nickname Jake in these circles.

Jake said, "That touches on the entire metaphysical debate that rages at times, and some neuroscientists and Bible-thumpers love to hate each other over it: whether normally-believed-in emotions like love, hate, sorrow, and joy are more real or if some underlying energy patterns as expressed by neurons and what-have-you are more real."

C.G.W. said, "You say put-on-Otto, and I say Tommy bought an igloo & an auto!! Whether or not an Otto Bismarck in the house picks up a Tommy gun and shoots you dead, whatever!"

There were a few seconds of – other than the background noise – stony silence in that area of the room.

C.G.W. continued with a little singing. "We all live in a Thompson submachine, a Thompson submachine, or, no, actually, we don't live in a giant submachinegun, do we?!"

Jake felt concern while continuing to silently contemplate the situation. Was C.G. Watts drunk out of his mind or getting borderline homicidal or both?

C.G.W. remarked, "Actually, I'm getting tired of this area of the room, including the mere act of having to look at your faces. You're starting to disgust me! I think I'll walk over there, I see some attractive young ladies who might make this a night to remember. Ciao!"

Jake watched as one Watts walked away and the other Watts remained. Both of them wondered whether Charlie Geronimo Watts was about to wreck his marriage, with a 17-24-year-old woman as an accomplice. Neither felt like bringing this up out loud on this occasion.

C.J. Soros felt like changing the subject. He inquired of Sammy Watts, "What do you think… really, most fundamentally… happened… under the surface during World War Two?"

Sammy requested some clarification, "Do you mean just during WW2 or both in the Nearly-Worldwide Great Depression's run-up to WW2 and through the war itself?"

Jake clarified, "Your opinion and thoughts, please, if you will, on the underlying forces and factors involving the entire 1920-1945 period."

Sammy looked for a moment like a dear caught in halogen headlights. Then he caught a gleam in his eye, closed both eyes for a second-and-a-half, reopened them, and resumed speaking, "Here's a mixture of stuff I know and stuff I conjecture. Some of it's ideas shared with others, and some might be me going out on a limb.

"There's something to be said for the idea in both Eastern mysticism and portions of Western mysticism... that some unified field of consciousness energizes and manipulates our entire freaking planet. Some strange stuff was a-happening to lead up to and cause WW1. Then Germany and some related places were beaten down so badly, it added fuel to the powder kegs that were already brewing up for centuries and millennia. Also, there's something about the occult. In many areas of academia, for whatever reason, the authorities, in their infinite wisdom, ban us from making much, *if any*, explicit reference to occult literature as sources for things like... I do not know a whole lot - excuse me - a whole lot about why the authorities in official academic circles for things like PhDs set things up to make the occult literature largely verboten for references, but this clearly has much to do with that.

"In any case. back there in Germany in the first half of the 20th Century, there were extreme explorations of the mysteries of the occult, of eastern philosophies, of western philosophies, of mysticism in general, and such. *They tapped into many of the primal energies.* They sought many of the greatest of truths, and they couldn't handle those truths very well. Therefofoooorrre, they sprang onto the world unspeakable horrors, th...   ...   ... through mixed intentions and insufficient character, integrity, and stuff with which to deal with those.

"Waiter, could I have some gin, please?" he asked a nearby waitress.

The waitress said, "I think you've had enough liquor for the night."

He said to her, "Lookey here." He thought about bringing out a bribe of $50 to get her to deem him sober enough to handle another drink, then thought better of it. A flashback to a youthful indiscretion when he was nineteen and a girl was seventeen and prone to impulsiveness, resulting in a long recovery period for him, came to mind. "Verbotene Experimente! Erlaubte Experimente!

"How about a cold-brewed coffee spiked with a little Dr. Pepper and Canada Dry Ginger Ale, plus a mystery ingredient of the bartender's choice? There could be a special tip for you to get a grip on!"

She said, looking him in the eye with sudden kinky intent, "Sure, it's coming right at ya, if you think you can handle what we might do with it, cowboy."

He looked into her eyes and felt temptation mixed with a twinge of concern about maintaining his marital vow of fidelity. He started leaning toward disaffection toward his vows, then leaning back toward affection toward his vows, then back and forth internally at a rapid pace.

Jake snapped his fingers and stomped his right foot.

Sammy snapped out of his temporary flash of lust toward the waitress. Remotely, at exactly the same time, C. Geronimo Watts snapped out of a temporary flash of lustful disregard for his marital vows.

Sammy said, "That waitress will probably be someone's lover tonight, but she won't be mine, because I'm gonna honor my wife. Well, back to whatever I was talking about, what was it?"

Jake said, "You were presenting some sort of grand unification hypothesis about just what the hell went down with the combos leading to the second world war."

Sammy continued, "Oh yes, thanks for the reminder. Where was I? Hmm, yes, yes."

He chuckled and grinned, then proceeded. "At some stages, some primitive us-versus-them mentalities set in. Elsewhere, in Japan and Italy, similar dynamics in some ways, and very different dynamics in other ways, *made also for the tapping into primal energies*, together with idiosyncratic character flaws ... ammo... amonga... among many of the principal players… people at or near the tops of the key power-house organizations in those places.

"Perhaps the us-versus-them mentalities are so fundamental to who we are as human beings… that no matter what we do or think, and no matter how much we intend for some great love toward everyone to make things like some utopian vision, the reality of our dark sides will complement the realities of our bright sides, and in the long run, extreme warfare is probably inevitable.

"Yet there was something *so different* about that one. Hmm, it's such a delicate matter how and if to say what I'm kind of thinking right now. Well, what the hell, here goes: It sure seems sometimes like a bunch of the Germans, Italians, and Japanese, for many different motives, coalesced into willfully and deliberately trying to be the catalyst for an apocalypse of all religions, sciences, and politics, to change everything around them, out of a profound disgust toward much of what the human race had become. In many ways, they succeeded in creating an apocalypse, though not much turned out anything at all like what they would have wanted."

"Interesting theory," said Charlie J.S.

The waitress, whose name was Sharisa Gertrude Neumann, and who presented herself to patrons as Cheryl G. Newman (including having business cards by that name for a side hustle of being a part-time life coach at $55/hr), had never met Charlie Geronimo Watts' wife Cheryl Nobel or Sammy Watts' wife Cheryl Shirley Watts.

Elsewhere at the party, a stiletto-wearing woman came within one psychic millimeter of choosing to kick a horny masher in the groin, yet said to him, instead, "You pathetic nerd. I don't want anything to do with physical contact with you, and I'm not interested in anything about you in any shape or form, and, if you reach out and touch me now or anytime in the future, I might kick you so hard that it makes you bleed down there and maybe winds up emasculating you forever!" She walked away from him, and immediately became hit upon by another masher. This time, in contrast, she felt attraction and affection for the masher, due to differences of physical characteristics and and zones of awareness and said, "Although you've been many places before, I dare you to drive me to Surfside Beach tonight, where we can spend some time alone together."

The woman thought for a brief flash at some semiconscious level, "What if the dandy and the buster know each other and are close friends? If they suddenly turn misogynist and team together, then I might be about to be raped or killed or maybe both. Hmm, what of it, I'll take my chances. The jock I'm walking out with is so gorgeous, so cute, so to-die-for!"

She, an hour-glass figured vixen, nevertheless, took a brief restroom break to double-check that her pepper spray, switchblade, cork, and razor blade were in her purse, in case useful later that night. Her father had served in combat in Vietnam and told her of how the combination of cork and razor could sometimes combine with female anatomy to deliver gruesome cases of men bleeding out. She hoped that she would never have to use that on a man, yet she sometimes wondered about how terrible a guy's behavior would have to be for it to justify for a woman to do that to him. Some would think the mere fact of being on the other side of war would justify such catastrophic luring, yet others would think that without a more substantial reason to do that to the male anatomy, it would be an even worse violation of the male anatomy than the rape of the female anatomy, unless the rape of the female anatomy were performed with a bayonet or another weapon of that extremity, which could be equally gruesome to how a concealed cork and razor can sometimes slice a man open lengthwise where and when he finds himself engorged with too much passion.

Returning to her normal thought patterns, she soon went out of her way to get Karen, one of her closest friends, to photograph her with her new male acquaintance, just in case he did in fact turn out to be the last person any of her friends would ever see her with alive.

While the hour-glass-figured lady with deep thoughts on blood and gore and humanity was in the restroom, the buster masher walked over to the dandy masher and asked, "You suggested this teamwork approach, that it's a risky human experiment we live in and we should just go for it with the situation. Maybe, I'm kind of ugly, and you're kind of handsome, but I'm still glad we premeditated some scenarios including this one."

The dandy replied, "Yes, I am, too! Hey, don't sell yourself short. Maybe many ladies might find me a seven or an eight and find you in the three or four range, but there are also many different ladies with different preferences. To some of them, you might even be above average! Also, if you can charm them with humor or common interests that could make you more attractive."

"You know what, our experiment is turning out even better than I thought so far. Quick, before she sees us together on good terms, which might lead her to telling me to get lost, here's an Andrew Jackson, a Thomas Jefferson, and two George Washingtons. Now scram!!"

The buster walked away hurriedly, suddenly $24 the richer.

A nearby caddie, owing no duty to either of them and having never met them before the party, laughed at them both, then received a dirty look from the dandy. The caddie immediately walked away, but not before returning the favor with a dirty look of his own aimed with looking the dandy right in the eyes. For a moment, Karen feared that the two men might come to blows, yet they showed restraint as the caddie went straight to his vehicle, drove home, then committed a triple homicide.

Nearby, the similarly-surnamed non-relatives Rogers Miles Busch and Roger Godfrey Bush were sharing a conversation unlike anything else anyone had ever seen.

Rogers asked, "One of the big controversies in some circles this year has been whether cell phones cause brain cancer or not. What do *you* think about whether they're a significant cause of *that*?"

Godfrey answered, "The jury's still out on that for *me*. What do *you* think?"

Rogers stated, "I think there's gotta be *at least a little* bit of a carcinogenic effect from it, yet it's very uncertain whether this would jump *over* the hurdle of materiality."

Godfrey said, "So, the jury's still out for you, as well!" He burst into derisive laughter, expressing a not-so-subtle disgust with all forms of affected sophistry.

Rogers looked at his conversational partner, *then* looked out *into empty space*, then *rocked* everyone, saying, "What's more interesting is the advancement of these devices and how they're only just beginning to transform the modern world.

"Many years from now, they'll reach more and more advanced stages. I wouldn't be surprised if people start talking about them in terms of here's fourth generation wireless technology, here's fifth generation, etc. But what of how hundreds of millions of years ago there were so many sail-backed, four-legged animals? Nowadays, few sizable land-dwellers have sails on their backs. Of course, with something of a parallel to how occult literature is largely banned from use in academic journals and college textbooks, what I'm about to say is essentially unprintable in our official paleontological papers, but I'll say it anyway. What if those sail-backed creatures, in addition to the official scientific-community-approved theories of why they had large sails, actually had them as evolved-to-be-built-in 'biological telepathy amiplifiers?' What then?"

With a matter-of-fact tone, Roger Godfrey answered, "Eleventh Generation wireless biotech, long before humans' first generation wireless anything."

Chapter Two: Synapsids and Reptilians in Portions of the Pennsylvanian and Permian Periods, Part I

It was spring, somewhere that would later be part of what humans call "Texas," 274,578 millennia and three weeks before The Tunguska Event. A young dimetrodon named Tryrordian Glinko telepathically intitiated a strong transmission toward a middle-aged dimetrodon named Sterling Lovecraft Jenkeysianson. Both were male, and they were at a distance of about five miles.

Tryrordian thought toward Sterling, "The food supplies here are running sufficient to maybe slightly insufficient, yet I have at least temporarily lost all interest in food. What are you up to at this time?"

Sterling picked up the signal and correctly sensed it through the ether. He responded, "I'm doing fine, thanks for asking. Just before your call, and, even now, multitasking with your telepathic call, I've been and am reading portions of the cave carvings of Dimetrioskis Elbankovic, a bipedal humanoid visitor I met twenty years ago. He didn't seem to have nearly as strong telepathically abilities as we do, yet he was able to communicate much through vocals, gestues, paintings, and carvings. Of everyone I've communicated with and myself, as a collective group, we are not entirely certain whether he was an extraterrestrial alien, an apparition, a time traveler, or something else. The same goes for the other seven bipedal humanoids publicly known to have visited us over the millions of years up to now.

"Years ago I glanced at some of this stuff on the walls of the cave, and it looked like it might involve alien conceptualizations of visitors from the other side of the sun or elsewhere in the heavens, yet it's making more sense now. Some possibilities are that deep in the future, there will be a great civilization, a great war, destruction, rebuilding, and new cycles of this sort of stuff. He had an epic vision, communicated in scenes and symbols."

Tryrordian said, "My family recently adopted an infant orphan. We are debating what to name him. I'm going to suggest that instead of giving him the surname "Glinko" my family should consider giving him the surname 'Elba,' like the beginning of 'Elbankovic.'"

Sterling responded, "Yes, I wholeheartedly agree that you should recommend that."

The Glinko family ended up naming the orphan infant *of unknown origins* Ion Elba. Many generations later, in the chain of male lineage, there emerged Dimetrio Elba, born on December 25th, 274,504,003 BCE. He would prove to be the longest living dimetrodon. That is: as measured by scientifically-observable spatio-temporal, biological-historical-lifespan standards of *the usually silent majority of fundamental reality, who might otherwise be referred to as the transcendental beings.* He was, among dimetrdons, not a one-in-a-million being or a one-in-a-billion, he was of unique power, grace, and utter transcendence.

In what normally would have been the ages of youth and middle age, while others were busy reproducing or attempting to reproduce, he made limited attempts at reproduction, largely revolving around engaging in dimetrodonian tantric sexual encounters, with which to heighten awareness of reality by delaying or avoiding mundane full gratification during those encounters, in exchange for sex which connected his partners and himself with elements of the divine. Also, as the dimetrodons often declined to match up one-to-one for monogamous relations, there were frequent instances of not knowing who was descended from whom. In contrast with this, though one of his most ancient of forefathers, the aforementioned Ion Elba, had unknown parents prior to being christened with the individual name Ion *and* the surname Elba by the Glinko family which adopted him, everyone in the chain from father to son to grandson and so forth had an essentially iron-clad knowledge that they were of the same male lineage. Elba could *feel* the connection going back through multitudes of generations, all the way back to the distant Ion, who had lived to the age of 1,999 years, five months, and 27 days before dying from, of all things, a lightning strike right after publicly praying in the middle of a battle, "Lord, Ultimate Reality or Realities, to whatever degree expressing thyself as God or The Most Awakened One or Whomever or

Whatever Else, if 'tis best that I die very soon by lightning strike or any other means to supercharge our dimetrodon forces in fighting back a coalition of those attempting to annihilate us, as a sacrifice toward prolonging the survival of our species both for our sakes and the long-run soteriology and enlightenment of the beings of Earth, then so be it, go for it!" Then came the intense lightning strike and concomitant thunder, and as Ion Elba collapsed into death by his own consent with the almighty, one hundred million enemy combatants suddenly themselves died by spontaneous animal combustion. This was one of the most controversial moments in the pre-ancient history of the planet. Although there were reptilians on both the side of Ion Elba and the dimetrodons and reptilians on the side Charr Naerroan and the igweolintians...

The Igweolintians (capitalized in the context of being citizens of the nation-state Igweolintus, lower-case in the context of being any shape shifters who at a given time was a true believer in the religion known as Igweolintu) had a fierce loyalty to a generally rigid authoritarian structure, and the theocratic government that jointly ruled both Igweolintu and Igweolintus. Although an overwhelmingly high percentage of the time witnessed the citizens of that nation believing in the state-sponsored religion, there were exceptions. The religion and the government sanctioned killing such heretics by any and all means. However, of these heretics as judged by the leaders of that religion, some had, around the year 276 million before the common era, found affinity with some of the diverse religions promulgated by various dimetrodons, cavarinksians, turnatorindians, edaphosaurs, and other sail-backed creatures. One of the main sticking points of disagreement involved the role of the planet Jupiter in the cosmos.

Dimetrodon and Edaphosaurian religions had interpretations of the consciousness or lack thereof, unity-of-consciousness or nonunity thereof, and wakefulness or thereof somehow happening with that planet as a whole, and these religions pointed all over the place with respect to what was allegedly real or not regarding Jupiter. In stark contrast, Igweolintu had a central tenet that planets like Jupiter -

gaseous giants, that is - spend most of their lives in a state of slumber, sometimes dreaming and sometimes in dreamless sleep. Then, when the ultimate reality itself, on occasions when the stars would all align, chooses to waken one or more gaseous giant in a given solar system and temporarily unify with its consciousness to deliver judgment to an entire planet. The igweolintians had somehow preserved within a sense of ancestral memory and symbolic mythology records that the Earth had a previous mass extinction and that similar planets in other solar systems had undergone multiple mass extinctions. To the vast majority of edaphosaurs and dimetrodons these were matters of conjecture, but a few of them also retained a sense of those ancestral memories and symbolic mythologies. Most shape-shifting reptiles and synapsids respected both sides of the conflict, some of the non-shape-shifting synapsids and reptiles respected both sides, and mammals were mainly meek beings trying to survive and bide their time for the future, often not yet ready to even understand or engage in deep levels of religion, science, and technology.

The religions of the dimetrodons, edaphosaurs, and turnatorindians included diverse and in many ways either superficially-contradictory or wholly-functionally-contradictory (at a given collapsing of quantum fields) religions, much like humans of future eons would include Mithraism, Jainism, Judaism, Sikhism, Buddhism, Christianity, Hellenic Pantheism, Hellenic Panentheism, Islam, Hinduism, and Himalayan hybrid religions. In contrast, Igweolintu resembled a highly-militarized, highly-judgment-day oriented hybrid of all of the aforementioned, with plenty of astrophysics weaved together with Papussian conceptualizations of the Tetragrammaton thrown in to boot. Before ancient Sumerians and Hebrews had, with varying degrees of success, attempted to harness the powers of the Tetragrammaton, a few Dimetrodonian religious practitioners and a few Igweolintian religious practitioners had already harnessed it, often to great effect.

Multitudes of surface-dwellers, though, knew not the degree to which the helicoprian sharks, other species of sharks, and various octopi would subtly play them off of each other through primitive means of remote influence. Sometimes the entirety of life in the oceans would unify as one super-consciousness that would wrestle with the entirety of life above the surface of the waters. Earthlife above the waters would only on exceedingly rare occasions be able to unify as one super-consciousness with which to wrestle back. It was of the days of Pangea.

Against the backdrop of that wild and nearly-totally-forgotten world, Dimetrio Elba maintained the health of an illness-free middle-aged living organism into what most would have presumed to be old age. He just kept living and living, while all of his contemporaries, in terms of dimetrodons and edaphosaurs, eventually succumbed to various deaths, one after another. After a while, public word got out among both the edaphosaurian and dimetrodonian communities that Elba had become the oldest living being they knew of in existence. Even more years went by, and intelligent beings of that "prehistoric" era reached a consensus that he was truly the elder of elders in their community.

By his 2,525th birthday, he had become more than a living legend, he was revered as perhaps the greatest being to have ever walked the surface of the planet, deified by some and nearly deified by others both for his mind-boggling longevity and for his interdisciplinary theological, scientific, and engineering accomplishments. Long before humans would build great pyramids in what would become Africa and the Americas, teams of dimetrodons and other living quadrupedal sail-backed biological beings used psychokinesis, telepathy, and telekinesis to construct an engineering marvel of a city-state in portions of what would later become known to human beings as "Siberia." One of the great engineers and architects of that city state, which was known to the dimetrodons and some of the other highly-intelligent living creatures of Earth as Siberia, was Evgeny Serling. Another was, indeed, Dimetrio Elba. Some considered it hard to say who had more vril-prints on the city, yet with Evgeny being one of the protégés of Dimetrio. On a related note, Evgeny's wife, Svetlena Serling, happened to be among Dimetrio's protégées, though the understudy males (i.e., protégés) greatly outnumbered the understudy females (i.e., protégées) in this case.

A few beings of those days would once in a while unintentionally teleport. They would also, in some very rare cases intentionally teleport. This was without the aid of official teleportation mechanical equipment, but through a conjunction of biology, mind, and higher-dimensional space, time, and space-time.

Prior to Dimetrio Elba's leadership, great swathes of dimetrodons had been in-fighting for millions of years about the controversies of religion, philosophy, science, and art. However, scores of millions of years before a man reputed to have born in Karkiv (in 1878 CE/AD as per most official records and questioned as by other records as to having been born either in 1877 or 1878 CE/AD and bearing a name that some would render) as Pyotr Demianovich Ouspensky would create a book (that would go on to be) called *Tertium Organum: The Third Canon of Human Thought, A Key to the Enigmas of the World*, the dimetrodon Dimetrio Elba created an extremely similar work titled *The Restoration of Ancient Integrative Consciousnesses*. Also, long before the perhaps-most-legendary of bipedal bio-organisms, Padmasambhava, created a magnum opus known to many as *The Tibetan Book of The Dead*, Dimetrio Elba created a somewhat similar work titled *How Beings of Any Numbers of Limbs Might Transcend the Unknowns of This and Other Realms*. Additionally, that very elderly Elba, after the loss of over 99.988% of the dimetrodon population from 274,501,478 BCE to 252,000,008 BCE, enacted a plan to steer the future of reality toward the possibility of the emergence of the intelligent mammals later known as dolphins, orca, and humans.

A REVISED INTERMEZZO BETWEEN Chapters 2 & 3: SELECT
EXPRESSIONS OF GRATITUDE AND DEDICATION:

Here are some of those without whom this work would most certainly not have
turned out to resemble anything close to what it has become:

  GM Garry Kasparov (of whose existence I became very aware circa September
1993)
  I finally met and shared a brief one-to-one conversation with him on January
27th, 2016, after he delivered a public speech that included a question-and-answer
session, mainly regarding geopolitics.
  To the best of my knowledge, up to the time of my composing this novel,
01/27/2016 was the only day in history that Garry Kasparov and I were at the
same venue at the same time.

  Liza Darnton (one of my Duke University "Introduction to Modern Philosophy"
classmates during the Spring Semester of 1995, and, with whom one-to-one
communication has been a rarity since)
  Such electronic communication subsequent to that semester has, at the visible
level, been almost entirely one-sided, with her *only directly observable* one-to-one
response since then... being *that she did choose to join networks with me* on one of the
online platforms on June 19, 2022 after I invited her.

  David "Godot" Hoffman (whom I first met circa September 1994, and *with whom
I am often still in a degree of regular contact* via social media)
  He and I met in person on many occasions from 1994-1998 in North Carolina and
again several times over the span of a few days in the third quarter of 2004 in
Connecticut in connection with fellow Duke alumnus Roger Wistar's wedding.
  One time he invited me to be among a group of men who gathered in Charlotte
to play street hockey. That was during the summer break of 1995 (relative to
university arrangements), and I accepted, and we enjoyed the team sport which,
to clarify, on that occasion included wearing normal athletic shoes.

  ...

  Tony "The Roofer" Holubik {more technically, Anthony Holubik II}
(whom I first met in early January of the year 2022 at a Starbucks, on a frigid
Houston morning, and who, like me, *is* in some literal sense "a military son," or in
other words, "among the sons of military service members")
  For clarification, being "a military son" in that sense *does not necessarily mean*
being "a military son" in the sense of "being an extremely hawkish person."

Therefore, although there are senses in which I can make any of the following four statements in ways that are reasonably truthful:

1. I am a military son.
2. I am not a military son.
3. Anthony Holubik II is a military son.
4. Anthony Holubik II is not a military son.

Yes, there have been many occasions on which Tony the Roofer and I have been hawkish in our dealings with other people, and, yes, there have been a few occasions that he and I have been hawkish with each other.

However, consider this observation: All sentient beings can, given enough capabilities, exemplify coordination of both dovish behaviors and hawkish behaviors in a manner that *does actually match* what is called for, when it is called for, and how it is called for... *echoing ancient wisdom literature,* both East and West.

...

Dorsey Armstrong (who taught the University Writing Course section that I attended at Duke University in the mostly-Autumnal-season Semester of 1994, which was the initial semester of my baccalaureate studies)

...

GM Sheng-yen Lu (with whom I shared a brief, nonverbal, one-to-one, mutual half-bow "conversation" one day near the middle of 2006 at a dining venue in Texas, and among whose live empowerment-ceremony audiences I was a member on two of the days in 2008 in Washington, on one of the days in 2009 in Texas, and on one of the days in 2011 in Texas)

...

...

...

...

Jessica "Let Me Tell You about the Movie *The Diving Bell and the Butterfly*" Trend (whom I met on May 6 and 11, 2011, and who last shared a live two-way conversation with me near the end of November in the year 2013, with that last conversation having been a reasonably amicable telephone call, though with intention to avoid planning future meetings)

The first time she and I met was on 5/6/2011 and totally unplanned by her and me, as we were previously oblivious to each other's existence. She and I happened to be browsing the same section of the Borders Bookstore that was in Meyerland Plaza in Houston, and we started talking about books and movies. She revealed that she had studied in the state of Maryland in the hopes of someday becoming a professional speech pathologist, yet things led her to working as a substitute teacher.

The November 2013 phone call included several revelations, not the least of which was that, although she had been single when she and I dated on 5/11/2011, she had subsequently become married. She and I mutually avoided contact for years, without having to resort to any official ban on contact.

All of a sudden, in March 2021 or thereabouts, I chose to call her 2011-2013 phone number. Though I have been generally of very limited verbal capabilities outside the English language, on that occasion I brought together portions of formulations from others in a composite outside of anything that anyone had ever directly told to me about anything and left Jess a multilingual voicemail... which some Twenty-First-Century scriveners might transcribe as resembling:

"Eadamu-, …

… …

父, 母,

Adam,

Iupiter, Zeus,

Deus, Иисус, Yeshua…

…

Om वज्रसत्त्व, Ah, Hum, Pei!

Om, Allahu Akbar, Adonai."

Please bear in mind regarding that the woman whose name this book renders as "Jessica Trend" in print: I never received clear and distinct confirmation of her name's spelling, however, for the sake of convenience, I have recorded it here to be spelled the way that it intuitively sounds like it is most likely to be spelled.

Last, but not least, I wish to thank three individuals who have been and are most likely long-term homeless Houstonians in the times leading up to and including the October 2022 publication of this work:

- "Meridian da Vinci" (a woman whom I met briefly on September 8, 2022)

On that day I bought a meal at Pho Zen Vietnamese Noodle House while conducting research presumably conducive toward novel writing. I discovered during that lunch the news that Queen Elizabeth II (21 APR 1926 to 8 SEP 2022) had died. Afterward, on a nearby sidewalk I met a woman who claimed to be named "Meridian da Vinci," she was moderately surprised to learn about Elizabeth II's death. The sidewalk conversation briefly and respectfully focused on that departed queen, then shifted to Meridian telling the tragic tale of how she had worked as a nurse, sometimes resided in Chapel Hill, NC, sometimes resided in Houston, TX, and lost both her job *and* her professional references when her former workplace *had a sudden run of death*, wiping out both the job and the references. That had made things extra difficult for her, part of a chain reaction that resulted in her homelessness.

She and I discussed philosophy, religion, neuroscience, health, metaphysics, and additional things, while in public view on the North Side of Westheimer Road, somewhere between Gessner and Tanglewilde. She mainly continued to sit mostly still in the sun. I often paced slightly back and forth as part of gathering thoughts.

On a few occasions since then, I have seen her hanging around the Midwest / Woodlake / Briarmeadow region of Houston, yet I have in the long run chosen to severely limit the amount of sharing conversation with her, as it became abundantly clear after a while that she would consistently and heavily gravitate toward focusing on tragedy, death, illness, and misfortune whenever speaking about reality, much more so than about 99.9% of people.

In a very different context, during portions of the late-September-to-early-October-2019 period I had briefly received the nickname Cul De Sac, presumably due to at least one other person perceiving me to have been obsessed with stuff outside mainstream culture. I have learned to let go of that obsession to a significant degree.

In contrast, I do not know, as of September 24, 2024, whether or not Meridian has to any significant degree let go of her previously-demonstrated tendency of obsession with tragedy and death.

On another note, the Pho Zen restaurant eventually closed, and, at the very location where it had been, the Pho Basil restaurant opened. That is near the Northwest corner of the intersection of Gessner and Westheimer in Houston, Texas.

•   Oden Giffin (a man whose name's pronunciation sounded like it could have easily been spelled "Odin Giffen," yet who, quite a while into our conversation in the afternoon of September 10, 2022, at my behest, clarified that it is legally spelled as shown at the beginning of this paragraph)

   He and I shared a dining experience at the Burger King on the South Side of Westheimer Rd not far from where I had met the aforementioned Meridian about 47 hours earlier.

•   Andrew Dane Mireles (a man whom I met several times in the second half of 2021 on and near portions of Westheimer Road significantly East of the region where I would meet Meridian and Oden in September of the following year)

   During that conversation with me, he pronounced his surname the way that people often pronounce "Morales," yet he made clear that the aforementioned rarity of a spelling as the correct one in his case. A transcript conveying the essence of part of a conversation between that A.D.M. and this M.J.B. forms part of the Epilogue.

Maurice James Blair
Houston, Texas, U.S.A.

   September 12-20, 2022, September 20, 2024, and September 24-26, 2024.

Chapter Three: Synapsids and Reptilians in Portions of the Pennsylvanian and Permian Periods, Part II, and Select Additional Highlights from Both The Paleozoic Era and The Mesozoic Era

About 300 million years before the Tunguska event that preceded the Great War, diverse creatures flourished on Earth. There were early fish, early sharks, octopi, squid, crustaceans, and others in the waters of the planet. In some sense there was just one main land mass and just one main ocean.

On land and in the air, giant insects, medium reptiles (whom some human scientists would refer to as being among the reptilians, also known as the saurians), medium reptile-like synapsids (who were more closely related to mammals than reptiles, although often appearing similar to reptiles), small mammals (who also were synapsids), and arachnids did dwell.

At some stage within the next few million years, there emerged, *from the merger of two different species*, the *early dimetrodons*. Physically evaluating the billions of years of development of biological entities, human scientists of the time of World War One and the one hundred four years after it would typically conclude that those beings of large sails and four legs, with two main types of teeth, were sophisticated for their time, yet no match for the sophistication of modern humans.

Something that most of the modern human beings as of the years 2021 and 2022 of the common era had missed *was* how both the dimetrodon beings and the edaphosaurus beings of yester-eon could harness heightened extrasensory perception capabilities through the use their sails.

A related note: Many modern scientists believe that it is impossible - or nearly impossible - for two species to have a partial merger with which to create a new species as an evolutionary process, *even defining the boundaries between species by making this a tautological exclusion from reality itself*, yet *it happened anyway*, way, way back when, *to result in the dimetrodons*. The edaphosaurs, in contrast, emerged by the much more astronomically-probable-and-normal evolutionary method in which one species evolves from one other specific species.

One of the things confusing to casual observers of paleontology is that some of the reptile-like synapsids have names with -saurus in them; *for example, specimens of the Edaphosaurus beings could be referred to as Edaphosaurians, though they were among the synapsids rather than the saurians.* Edaphosaurus beings were generally either herbivorous (or in rare cases omnivorous), whereas the similar-looking Dimetrodon beings were generally either omnivorous or carnivorous, depending on individual preferences and circumstances. Human scientists would later believe it overwhelmingly most likely that Edaphasaurus beings were monolithically herbivorous and that Dimetrodon beings were monolithically carnivorous, yet the realities of yester-eon were often much less monolithic than generally reflected by the conventions of mid-Twentieth- to early-Twenty-First-Century academia. Dimetrodons were often the planet's main land-dwelling alpha predators during much of the 280-millions B.C.E. and the 270-millions B.C.E.

As described in the preceding chapter, some forms of advanced technology were already present in our world among many beings of the period from 252 million to 292 million years before what many historians call The Dorian Invasion. Over the span of a number of decades in the Twentieth and Twenty-First Centuries A.D./C.E., various resources expressed different demarcations of time to reflect what timings were for the beginnings and endings of the Permian and Pennsylvanian periods. To whatever degree scientific researchers have accurately or inaccurately characterized events that transpired from 350 million years before the Year 2022 (as measured by the Gregorian Calendar) to 220 million years before that year, their works have provided gateways into esoteric knowledge. Likewise, to whatever degree that fiction works about paleontology have chanced upon accurate or inaccurate characterizations or transcended exact relations with the concepts of accuracy and reality, they have provided gateways into absolute truths, relative truths, and the totally absolute.

Long before the ancient human nation of Sumer temporarily unified vital statics and dynamics of integration, differentiation, and transfiguration, to marvelous effect, the zones of awareness of living creatures *felt and knew* much of this *without having to conceptualize it*. After a while, in what many would call *pre-historic* times, some of the living things of the planet already achieved the tracking of *history*, through means of *telepathy, artifacts, and energy*.

Dimetrodonian technologies were at times pitted against Igweolintian technologies, as part of warfare that relied heavily on telepathy, psychokinesis, and the weaponization of large insects and golems. Although the reptiles were often fighting on both sides in the early days of the conflicts of that, as the millions of years rolled along the tide of reptilian loyalty shifted very much in favor of the Igweolintians.

When the wars of quadruped-versus-quadruped alternate notions of superiorities had reached their zenith in the year 270,000,000 BCE/BC, the climactic scene unfolded as follows:

Zircon Gilroy, a transformational reptile shapeshifter of indeterminate species (relative to early Twenty-First Century human scientific theories), teamed up with many reptiles of determinate species (relative to the aforementioned theories) to create military bases in Carthage and Bombay (which were, ironically or non-ironically enough), already known at the time - via selective telepathic transmissions - to both synapsids and reptilians as "Carthage" and "Bombay".

Reptilians versus Synapsids, with each side resorting to the full use of all religions, sciences, arts, and philosophies in concert, fought tooth and nail and dagger, extending both regular and telekinetic arts of warcraft to levels that the living humans of June 29th, 1908 CE/AD would have seldom dreamed possible.

The primary military bases of the synapsids were located in Siberia and what would later be called the Himalayan region. Regarding the latter, that military might had its most densely concentrated munitions housed in the region that would later be referred to by some humans as Kashmir. Humans of the third millennium of the common era, if able to travel back in time and telepathically tune into the various interspecies 11G biotelecommunications, would have noticed numerous religious and scientific methods identical to portions of physics, neuroscience, chemistry, mechanical engineering, *and even Abrahamic Religious methods, Brahmanic Religious methods, metaphysics, ethics, multireligious Dharmic philosophies, scientific methods, and Universalist Panentheism.* It was quite a time to be alive.

Quite a time to be alive, but maybe not so much for the faint of heart and the weary. One of the favorite weapons of choice by both sides were the insects. Although birds and proto-birds were exceedingly - yea, verily, even astronomically - rare on Earth until about 150 million years before the common era, large insects, such as the griffinflies (some of which, such as *Meganeuropsis permiana*, could have a wingspan about as wide as some housecats are long). Arachnids could also get big back then, as could Eurypterids. The ancient sea scorpion referred to as *Jaekelopterus rhenaniae* could at times achieve lengths greater than what would later become the heights of the tallest NBA players.

Through the use of prayers, blessings, curses, spells, mantras, and alternative practices, many of the non-insect-non-arachnid-non-eurypterid beings were able to genetically and behaviorally manipulate the way that insects, eurypterids, and arachnids would do what they do, siccing them on their opponents.

Additionally, there was widespread - and highly successful - willful manipulation of weather patterns. In particular, a few reptiles here and there and a few synapsids here and there could occasionally direct where and when lightning would strike.

On July 28th in the year 270 million before the common era, Carthaginian reptiles, some of their allies, and their minions prepared a fully functional atom bomb and set it aside within a vault for potential future use. However, it was left dormant for millions upon millions of years, in fact for well over 269.99 million years. It would go on to become part of a human shrine in Carthage, until a Carthaginian priest, in a desperate attempt to call on the help of divinity to assist defense against the Romans, accidentally detonated it in the year 202 B.C.

Back to July 28th, 270,000,000 B.C.E. Elsewhere, using astronomical multitudes of specialized insects, arachnids, and others as biological constructors of mechanical equipment, through modified 11G transmissions of mental activity through the ether and other means, physical military technology reached true greatness. It in general became similar to some of the World War Two level of human state-of-the-art capabilities.

Having weaponized much of their entire reality, a few brave souls dared to go even further, calling out with all their might toward whomever in the heavens - whether human, alternate biped, alternate quadruped, pure-energy, or hybrid beings, or, for that matter, anyone else - who should happen to hear their calls.

Some started new traditions focused on the bipedal humanoid as a class of beings who might someday save the planet from the oft-deadly synapsids-versus-reptilians holy wars and many other threats.

Some of the legendary names of potential humanoids who might someday prove helpful according to various of their prophetic traditions (bandied about amidst their seemingly-never-ending warfare) *were*: Samantabhadra, Samantabhadri, Tara, The Adamantine One, Adam, and Matsya.

There were many arguments among camps and subcamps of those ultra-ancient synapsids and reptiles about such things as whether 1) Adam and Matsya were representative of the same being or two different beings... or perhaps referring to three or seven or more beings, 2) whether God and Adibuddha are identical to each other or not, and 3) the degrees of reality or lack thereof of birth, life, death, afterlife, obliteration, reincarnation, and transfiguration.

However, many of those who felt the most despair plus some who felt the least despair and others did look toward the imagined possibility of the human form as a symbol of hope.

Both sides of that holy war (as alleged by some) or unholy war (as alleged by others), however, *whether for good or for ill*, somehow achieved the *wholesale "effective" delivery of biological warfare* upon their enemies by October 17th, 270,000,000 BCE. By November 9th of that year, the spread of illnesses and deaths was already extremely terrible across many parts of Pangea. By December 6th, 270,000,000 BC, the fighting temporarily halted, because both sides faced unforeseen mayhem as the biological warfare had proved several magnitudes of order more "successful" than they had planned.

Nevertheless, on or about December 14th of that year, a few skirmishes had restarted, and by January 31st the next year (relative to time measurements that would later prove popular through much of human civilization), widespread warfare had resumed. Still, bear in mind that it never again reached the zenith that it did on precisely the 17th Day of October in the Year 270 million BCE, with speech and actions that unleashed unspeakable openings of Pandora's boxes and other eschatological stirrings.

At least, that is, the zenith was surpassed not via reptilians versus synapsids. *Synapsid-versus-synapsid warfare*, some 270 million years and change later, found ways to - in the minds of many beholders - outdo that former *zenith* of *War on Earth and Ill Will Toward Over Half or Nearly All.*

After that, as Zircon and Dimetrio simultaneously transitioned into the beyond in a *sublimation* similar to how some later interpreted a human of the name Enoch to have *sublimated* out of worldly life without dying, they still continued their rivalry.

Both cared deeply about the spiritual enlightenment, wisdom, and agapic potential in all beings, though Zircon placed much less emphasis on agapic love and much more emphasis on wisdom, whereas Dimetrio had a more balanced emphasis on all three.

Almost 19 million years went by, seeing the near-extinction of dimetrodons and the near-extinction of the sea-dwelling eurypterids who performed many naval and marine operations on their behalf, as the Igweolintians' abilities to sway the vast majority of reptiles in their favor proved deadly to trillions.

Dimetrio suddenly had a flash of insight: He temporarily unified both the Dimetrodonian religious energies and the Igweolintian religious energies within the fibers of his being and channeled energies toward the planets Jupiter, Saturn, and Neptune, with full intent to bring all the accumulated karma of all time to land on everyone and everything. It was on December 31st, 251,108,001 BCE.

Suddenly, in the year 251,108,000 BCE, *the entire planet Jupiter* awoke from a 50-million-year hibernation, *shining the entirety of its collective planetary consciousness* upon Earth. The Planet Jupiter found *disgust* with *all life on the Planet Earth.*

Before Dimetrio and Zircon, *both of whom were dwelling somewhere between bardo states and full paranirvana,* even knew it had started, *Jupiter-as-a-whole telekinetically induced portions of Siberia to erupt a supereschatological supervolcano.*

...

Horatio Zlotnike and Deborah Goladolwa were the last two dimetrodons left among the historically living at that instant, and they were an offspringless couple. They lived in Texas, yet they *both* heard *and* felt, via their sails, ears, minds, hearts, and souls, from the other side of the world, emanations from what would prove to be the beginning of the end for trillions of quadrillions of the Earth's inhabitants.

Horatio said to his mate Deborah, "Oh, God, what was that noise! The terrestrial and ethereal transmissions just reached an overload!!"

Deborah stated, "*This is it*: deep within the preachings of both Dimetrio Elba and his nemesis Zircon Gilroy there are those prophecies that if neither side of the synapsid-vs.-reptilian holy war performs well enough their duties to the ultimate, then beings of the beyond will deem everyone on Earth to be excessively left-hand path, bringing down all the hammers of all the gods and The Vajra Dagger of Adi-Buddha God to deliver holy wrath upon all life on Earth. *I can't help but ff… ffeeeel thaaat… it's jj… just… started.*"

The couple looked into each other's eyes and telephathically communicated both romantic and agapic love, not knowing whether they or anyone else on Earth would have much longer to live. Nearby, a small flock of mostly-vegetarian sail-backed quadrupeds who lived on Horatio and Deborah's farm felt much the same way.

Susan Sherwood said to both Thomas Smirnoff and Jerry Grockenspree, "Our last remaining dimetrodon overlords probably know more about this than we do. However, it would be more polite to give them some more time to evaluate what it means, rather than barge in and ask what the hell they think and know about what's up with something huge that's happened in the distance."

Smirnoff replied, "To evaluate what it means, and to consider what to do next. I trust them, with their more advanced technologies, to usually make good decisions, even when they choose to euthanize some of us by, with or without our consent, transitioning us into the state of death and then feeding upon our carcasses. I trust them now to have a great chance to diagnose those rumblings from far away and do something constructive about them."

Grockenspree disagreed. He said, "There's some *unknown* reason why I feel like I *know* it. We're all about to die very soon. There will be little, if any, left of the world that we know. The survivors, if any, shall be the meek, and they will inherit a world that will have forgotten almost everything about the civilizations that now exist."

Susan and Thomas became motionless, though still wide awake. Jerry Grockenspree continued, "I don't know who or what is doing this to our planet, yet I truly believe this is the end of the God-damned war between the overly-dispassionate reptiles and the overly-passionate synapsids. That is, unless reptiles and synapsids somehow survive this disaster that's just begun, and live long enough to rekindle their rivalry in the distant future. As both of you know, I, *being an ultra-rare hybrid of synapsid and reptile,* find the absurdity of this instant... something that no words could do justice for. Maybe this is the God-blessed judgment day: The Ultimate landing It on us all."

Sherwood suddenly found the gumption to speak up. "How can you talk like that? Some of the legends from long before either Zircon or Elba were allegedly born into this world indicated that illusory manifestations of The Ultimate might be perceived as this or that version of God almighty and even called 'God almighty' by many beings, while still falling short of truly being The Ultimate.

"Some have even gone so far as to say that The Ultimate is so far beyond our ability to comprehend It that He or She or They or Whatever or Whoever is, in fact, even beyond every concept anyone could ever have of Gyod, God, G-d, Adibuddha, Tao, or any of the remaining conveyances of that absolute. Therefore, just because some will label this catastrophe a so-called 'Act of God,' it does not necessarily mean that it emanates directly from The Ultimate. It could be the act of an impostor who is not quite at the level of Adibuddha or God or what-have-you."

Grockenspree retorted, "To whatever degree that it emanates from The Ultimate or from someone or something that falls somewhat short of The Ultimate, it is what it is... and maybe in this case, it is something much more profound to reality as a whole than it is to merely us."

Smirnoff replied, "Like, duh! It has to be more profound than just what it is to us. Look in the distance. See the patterns in the skies. We've never seen armadas of aircraft of such huge numbers before."

A previously silent visitor, also a sail-backed quadruped, had walked in on the conversation at the time that Susan had begun to respond to Jerry. That silent visitor, named Lorentzia Dorian was a female synapsid of indeterminate species, and about seven-and-a-half centuries old, yet wise beyond her years. She said, "Those are not armadas of aircraft. *They are spacecraft.*"

Smirnoff disagreed. "Sensationalist, paranormal hogwash! How can anyone be so sure that spacecraft even exist? Many scientists, even today, conjecture that exiting the atmosphere of any given planet to venture into outer space is either a pipedream or something that will need to wait for millions more years of technical advancement. In the absence of strong evidence that these things in the sky came here from outer space, I believe it most prudent to presume that someone somewhere on Earth simply flew those things into the sky to gather here. What makes *you* so confident that it's otherwise?"

Lorentzia said, "Because, about a century ago, *I called on them* to come back, *and back they are.*"

Susan, Thomas, and Jerry *literally* turned to stone upon hearing and seeing this. Lorentzia proceeded to walk to near the outer perimeter of the farm. There she looked up to the armada and said, "Welcome back! I truly believe someone or something in this solar system is instigating an annihilation or a near-annihilation of all life forms on Earth. *What do you think?*"

A hologram of Adam Kadmon, Adam, Eve, Samantabhadra, Samantabhadri, and Noah appeared before her. They were silent for eight seconds, then Samantabhadra, Samantabhadri, and Adam vanished from the hologram presentation.

Another three seconds of silence from the presented hologram transpired, then Eve and Adam appeared to vanish.

Noah stepped closer and said, "*You called on us* 101 years ago today. *We communicated with you about an impending doom for your world.* We do not know for sure whether life on your planet will still be around one million years from now, let alone a-quarter-of-a-billion-years hence, but we invite you to step aboard *an interstellar interdimensional vessel.* We will now give you only one chance to answer this question. Do you agree to step aboard right now?"

Lorentzia answered with a resounding, "Yes!" She continued, "How do I step aboard?"

Noah said, "*Stand very still*. A helicopter will land about twenty yards from here. Three men and three women will walk to position themselves into a pattern in which you shall be equidistant from each of them, with yourself somewhat in the middle of a hexagonal pattern of humans. We shall then teleport all seven beings, that being a combination of yourself and the six people, aboard a starship. You are one of at least five million beings that our armada is attempting to frantically rescue from this potentially dying *world*."

Lorentzia stood as still as a British royal guard on a watch duty.

Soon, the six humans arrived, *not as holograms, but as actual persons in the flesh*. They did just as the Noah hologram said that they would, and the group of seven beings teleported aboard one of the vessels.

The armada succeeded in rescuing approximately 4.9 million of the inhabitants of Earth by interdimensional and insterstellar journeys aboard spacecraft. They also provided esoteric technologies to another 200,000 of the inhabitants left to mostly fend for themseleves amidst the supervolcanoes, greenhouse-gas shrouds, extreme climate change, and other tribulations.

By the time that The Great Dying had ended, extremely few of the previously inhabiting species of Earth were left alive. Some survivors carried an ancestral memory in their zones of awareness, a profound sense that seemingly almost everyone had gone extinct.

In many respects, it could be easy for sentient beings to interpret that life and technology in general had been set back between 200 million and 340 million years.

Throughout much of the Triassic period that ensued, multitudes of technological remnants of bygone eras were still visible on Earth in the form of artifacts.

Dinosaurs and early birds of the Mesozoic era had little inkling of the extreme cultures and technologies that had been present on the planet during the latter stages of the Paleozoic era. Nevertheless, they often operated as fierce and crafty gladitorial and nongladitorial participants of the dramas of life.

As pterosaurs, proto-birds, and birds started to have major prominence in the skies, there emerged major aerial combat between large insects, small-to-medium birds, proto-birds of various sizes, and pteresaurs. A lack of sufficient maneuverability among super-sized insects, together with the major reductions in the oxygen percentage in the atmosphere of the planet, led to the surviving insects in the long run shifting to size limits rather miniature by comparison with their old-time maximum sizes.

On land, in the seas, and in the skies, much of the combat still ended up serving as proxy fighting between beings who had passed into the beyond. Those beings who would at times die, disappear from reality, eventually reawaken (sometimes and to some degree by reincarnation and sometimes & sometimes and to some degree by reappearing as ghosts and other types of spirits), usually still did not know for sure about the ultimate answers to the questions of metaphysics and ethics.

What many of them did know, however, was that they did not feel ready to bury the hatchets of their old-time rivalries and bitter feuds.

Many then-living dinosaurs, proto-birds, birds, ocean-dwellers, insects, and arachnids, and other organisms of the Mesozoic, much like earthlings from the later portions of the Paleozoic, found themselves under the watchful observation and telepathic influence of Zircon Gilroy, Dimetrio Elba, and other beings of the beyond (who sometimes cooperated and sometimes competed against one other).

Deep underwater, on December 26th, 85,100,081 BCE, a five-year-old naga and a twenty-seven-year-old naga listened as several thirty-something-year-old nagas discussed the secret history of humans and posited hypotheses thereof:

Thirty-five-year-old William Encausse said, "Here's a vision of what I believe just might have happened long ago on the surface of our planet: The Ultimate Creator Deity bestowed upon earth nearly-infinite potential to support life. Then He transcended unity of being by differentiating portions of his essence into multiple male, female, and neutral-gender beings. After that, multiple cycles of transitions from unity to multiplicity and back to unity again unfolded. And here we are today."

Thirty-seven-year-old Alexander Einstein responded, "I am somewhat skeptical of that vision. Here's an alternate hypothesis: The Ultimate Creator somehow generated multiple universes, then, within this universe, set the stage for the possibility of human life and other intelligent life on many different planets within many different galaxies. Then She or He or It chose to sit back, with many very rigid ground-rules in place, and let things unfold, only intervening in the most extreme of circumstances. Human life, other than the small percentage of extraterrestrial visitors who are human, has not yet developed on this planet, but it might someday flourish."

William said, "Maybe these two visions are mutually exclusive, and maybe they're not, yet, either way, what about The Rods of God?"

Alexander said, "Yes, sometimes when I walk on land and sometimes when I fly in the sky I remember them more vividly than when I swim in the sea. Before I say much more about them, please retell some highlights of your encounters with them."

William enlightened the crowd via interwoven glimpses. "About three years ago, I was flying over Mount Kilamanjaro when I decided to go to higher altitude. Going higher and higher, I reached portions of the upper stratosphere. *Then they went flying by at about Mach 17.*

"They looked like giant cylinders, ranging from 24 meters to 500 meters in length."

"Another time, I flew over Mount Rainier. Lord Adibuddha, Good God YHVH, What the hell happened next?!

"I looked across the clouds and again saw Mount Rainier poking through the clouds with its summit looking like a rocky island in a sea of cloud-work. I had a flashback to an old news report conversation in which someone told another about those Rods of God. Although I did not see any of those Rods that time near that towering peak, I decided to take a five-month sabbatical from dwelling above the surface of the seas.

"After the sabbatical, I thought to myself, 'Where shouldst methinketh shouldst be the venue for my next flight?' Thence, removing myself from the relative safety of the seas, I chose to go straight from the ocean to the sky, and took off like a just-launched submarine-based intercontinental ballistic missile.

"Flying around a variety of ambivalent, inhospitable, and hospitable skyways here, there, and yonder, I found myself over Antarctica. What do you know, would you even believe it? About twenty five of those rods went zooming by so fast that I have no idea whether they were going at Mach 27 or Mach 227!!"

There came the thunderous underwater equivalent of revelatory applause. Alexander then returned to speaking. "Thank you for that rather stupendous storytelling! I'll add this about my experiences with those rods. *I'm in serious doubt about every theory we have about who or what they are and who or what causes them to arrive and move the way that they do.* Are they super-animals? Are they extreme aircraft? Are they spacecraft? Are they directly from the divine?

"Whichever the truth might be about the answers to these questions, I know I've seen them flying in the stratosphere at speeds that defy virtually all normal logic. I can corroborate William's description that they sometimes appear, as measured by radar, to travel multiple times the basic Mach 5 or thereabouts needed to reach hypersonic speed."

Chapter Four: 1,907 ½ Years Before The Tunguska Event, and The Day of That Event

On the night of what would later be classified by measurements of The Gregorian Calendar as used throughout The Twentieth Century (Anno Domini, vis-à-vis how Dionysius Exiguus and others arranged that calendar, and as some of those with a strong affinity toward Arthur Charles Clarke, Neil deGrasse Tyson and other heavily-science-oriented persons would at times find Common Era to be a more agreeable means of conveyance) as having been December 31st, 1 B.C. / December 31st, 1 B.C.E., being the day immediately preceding January 1st, 1 A.D. / January 1st, 1 C.E., something happened that should overshadow anyone's sense of distraction from the legalese-style calendaristic ravings of this sentence.

Although the demarcation of when one year changes to the next had ancient differences, with some people having the new year begin at the beginning of March, others using the end of June or July, and others doing other things with this, in modern times the main convention has been to have the calendar year begin with January 1st each year.

Using the modern measuring methods described above, there was something super-peculiar about the transition from December 31st of the Gregorian Calendar year one that was before the other Gregorian Calendar year one to the January 1st of the following year, which was itself also a year one: All over the world, essentially the entire human race, felt, to one degree or another, an inner feeling that usually never vanishes simply vanish into nothingness. This happened along the moving meridian at the midpoint of time between dusk and dawn - more technically in the 1/3,600th of 1/24th of one day (i.e., one second) from 11:59:59 PM to 12:00:00 AM, not as measured by any time zone(s), but as measured by the relationship between earth, sun, dusk, and dawn.

Although words could never fully do this justice by themselves, a given reader, writer, or other explorer could potentially tap into this with a degree of success by going beyond the words into imagining and tuning into feeling what these words are attempting to point toward.

Imagine this, if you would: You are moving along through your life, and you are used to a general feeling of the inner ecosystem of your energies within yourself, energies that could manifest at a given time through any combination of the presence or absence or quantum quasi-presence-quasi-absence of love, hate, joy, sorrow, confidence, lack of confidence, libido, lack of libido, lack of focus, focus, volatility, equanimity, etc. Other people are moving along through their lives doing much the same. Then, all of a sudden, there is an instant of time in which a major portion of that energy simply stops, somehow ceases to be. You start to talk with others about what happens, and, to the dismay of both the others and yourself, you find out that the loss of some of the subtle winds of inner being has happened for them as well. If this happened to people all over the world, some high though not absolutely 100% total of humanity, say, perhaps 95% or 99.3% of humanity, then, even if left off of official historical records, it would leave a lasting imprint on the psyches of the human beings anyway.

In many, though not all, of the universes described in this storyline, such an occurrence did indeed happen, at what would by Twenty-First Century measurements have been pinpointed as the last second of time of 1 B.C. / 1 B.C.E. into the midnight that transcends being in that year and the year after it. Some might say that midnight is technically in the new year, and some semantics can register this with the mind, yet others might say that midnight is technically something which transcends exactly being of this year or that year. As conventional geometry limits the definition of a given point to never having any adjacent points other than itself, then if we define midnight as belonging to the next day, then the last instant of time from the previous day is unobtainable in terms of ever becoming officially measured: If measured as midnight, then defined to be of the next day, if measured as prior to midnight, then defined to be of the earlier of the two days. Yet, as perhaps millions or quadrillions of beings have cognized previously, and some, such as P.D. Ouspensky in *Tertium Organum*, have directly or almost directly pointed out, any instant in time obtained prior to it would have *an infinite range of potentially obtainable instants in time between itself and the other instant in time.* Therefore, if midnight is itself unobtainably between the earlier of the two days and the latter, then the transitional instant between the days is identifiable as midnight; whereas, if midnight is defined as totally belonging to the latter day and not the former, then the last instant of time belonging to the former day is a forever-unobtainable instant that would under conven-tional geometry have to meet the self-contradictory requirements of 1) being prior to midnight, and 2) being precisely adjacent to midnight. This is a case the idea of what would otherwise be a typographic error between the word "semantics" (having to do with the controversies and alternatives of the convey-ances of words) and the word "sematics" (having to do with the awareness and risk managements of dealing with dangerous patterns of marking, including potentially-lethal consequences) could prove to have the two different words converge into mutual accuracy with a degree of interchangeability. Usually, the two would not be interchangeable and could cause writers and readers confus-ion shouldst they be unintentionally switched. However, in this case switching them, either intentionally or unintentionally, could still result in sentences that could readily make sense.

For example, consider two sentences, which differ by only one letter. First: "The semantics of the degree or degrees to which a given beholder considers midnight to belong to the new day versus the degree or degrees to which said beholder considers midnight to somewhat straddle and transcend the two days could lead such a reader down a logical rabbit hole from which he or she might not ever recover." Second: "The sematics of the degree or degrees to which a given beholder considers midnight to belong to the new day versus the degree or degrees to which said beholder considers midnight to somewhat straddle and transcend the two days could lead such a reader down a logical rabbit hole from which he or she might not ever recover."

Here is a third sentence, which under some interpretations has nothing to do with the prior discussion and under other interpretations has everything to do with the prior discussion: "The hard hand had a way of delivering harsh consequences to those who neglected to render unto dharma and karma that which they should have rightfully rendered unto dharma and karma."

* * * * *

A high percentage of the beings who died on Earth (to include the waters, the lands, and the atmosphere, and anywhere else) from about 251.9 million years B.C./B.C.E. to about 242.05 million years B.C./B.C.E., went straight to the mysterious state (or nonstate) of total obliteration nonbeing for seemingly eternity. However, as the comet approached Earth in late June in the year 1908 C.E./A.D., they transitioned *out of obliterated nonbeing into dreamless sleep deep unconsciousness and subtly-slightly-having-a-trace-of-consciousness subconsciousness, experiencing a degree of the bardo realm*, while, for reasons unknown to practically every being to have ever been in existence anywhere, *suddenly starting to hitch a ride on that comet.*

On June 30th, 1908, that comet struck Siberia, and *both nothing and everything* were delivered.

Chapter Five: The Ancient Dorians, Their Commitment to Death Before Dishonor, and Highlights from Their Conflicts with Those Whom They Believed It Their Duty to Destroy and Subsequently Rebuild

"How dare you tell me that I should not go on that journey to the big divine orgy party? The Mycenaeans invited Dorians, Hebrews, Remians, Teutons, and many others to join in a festival of both sensuality and spirituality! They said they will finally be revealing to outsiders many of their long-kept secrets, for the good of all mankind!" exclaimed Petrus Onassis to his girlfriend Pattyla Heraclisseus.

Pattyla responded, "Petrus, my dear, if I had a good feeling about this whole affair, I would say, 'My love, I totally agree with you fervently, let's both go! I would love for us to try out many different partners in a swingers jamboree combined with learning many religious secrets! Let's go, then after we've tried this out for a while and returned safely to our Dorian homeland, we'll find out if our relationship is strong enough to withstand such a wild three-week party. Let's do this!!'

"You see, not only am I not all-in on this adventure, I've got a strong feeling in almost every fiber of my being that this is not going to end well for anyone."

Petrus retorted, "Oh come on! Love is how we expand our horizons, fear is the way we attract negativity. I believe you should trust this process more!"

Pattyla already saw this coming. "Look, if you think less with your dick and more with your brain, you'll recognize that there is great value in both the Chessed of loving-openness toward all and the Gevurah of stern gravity toward the very real dangers and risks we face as living beings. Sure, we might not always know all that well when to do what with whom, but we should listen to our feelings and *often trust* our intuitions about how to decide what to do, what not to do, when to do or not to do, and such. *All of my intuition seems to point in the direction of screaming to me that the mixture of goodwill and ill-will between Mycenaeans and Dorians, together with everything else about love and sex and orgies and spirituality is about to explode.* Explode destructively, that is.

"If we go to that event, or if you go to that event without me, either way, this is going to be like volunteering to swim with sharks and barracuda and extraterrestrials while skinny dipping. Or maybe that's not the best analogy.

"How about this one: Someone's built a large straw house next to a large wooden lodge. Then a bunch of folks are invited to a séance to be held there, and it's BYOC: bring your own candles. So you have lots of people carrying candles and some even carrying full-blown torches into highly-flammable buildings.

"What could go wrong?!" she said, smirking with sarcasm. She was left-handed, whereas Petrus was right-handed, by the way.

She immediately bit down somewhat hard on the middle finger of her left hand, then released, revealing intentional slight imprints from her teeth.

"I love it when you do that!" Petrus said with a grin. "And that's part of why I believe that you should relent and not only give me a blessing to go there, but join me over there! Sure, we've had our thrills with each other, and so far so good, but I feel that we could do better with the consistency of pushing the envelope of pleasure and pain and thrills! You're a great gal, and I love you, but about three-fourths of the time, you're more inhibited than I want you to be!"

Pattyla shook her head slightly, then performed a half-nod. She then partially shook her head again before looking him right in the eyes and presenting a heartfelt message. "Yes, and about two-thirds of the time, I find you way too unhibited!!

"You're a great guy, truth be told, fun to be with, and I love you, yet you're… often about one misstep away lately… from getting… destroyed. Maybe partway or totally destroyed between your legs or maybe getting destroyed between your ears, or maybe just plain totally killed, whether by a lover or a friend or a foe.

"It's one thing to be brave, but it's another to be so thrill-seeking that you play Russian roulette with your soul, your heart, your mind, and everything else you've got."

Petrus inquired, "What's Russian roulette?"

Pattyla answered, "Maybe you're the first person I've used that phrase with since learning it about six or seven years ago, at a time when I was a fourteen-year-old and Brenda was eighteen years old.

"On that day, seemingly eons ago, my sisters and I took a shortcut through a forest. We wandered and became confused, as our compasses started to go haywire.

"At some point, we stumbled upon a peculiar-looking elderly gentleman who spoke our language, though with only about 75% fluency. He offered a quid pro quo: for one dance with my sister Brenda, he would transport us to a wondrous place with technologies beyond our dreams for about half an hour, then transport us back to the outskirts of our home town of Suitsterbyeulis. Not only did Brenda dance with him, after a little while she and he seemed to fall madly in love, and they made passionate love, right there in front of me and my other sisters Karyellenyia and Suellena. In case you're wondering, no, I and the other two sisters did not make this into a ménage à trois or something even further.

"After the five of us walked to a stream and the two lovers bathed as the rest of us lightly freshened up, the gentleman said we should stand still, vey still. He picked up from his right-front pocket some sort of device and spoke in a foreign language. Soon a large mechanical bird with two sets of rotating bladed wings landed. The two men on board indicated that there was plenty of room for us to board, and board we did. We flew away in that rotating-bladed-winged flying creature. Such a strange creature! We went up into the sky and soon landed in a place that they called 'Vietnam." They said it was 'The Year Nineteen-Sixty-Eight,' whatever that might mean. My sisters and I got to hang out with some people with super-advanced technologies. I asked about the foreign language, and he said it was called 'American English.'

"Most of them did not speak our language, a few of them could communicate a few lines here and there, and just one of them, the weird guy who helped bring us there, a Sgt. Norman Petty, showed us a presentation of Russian roulette.

"There was this machine, it had reams of still-frame images on miniature things, all lined up. It ran through a thing with a lamp in it, and out from the lamp-thing with the spinning reams came a shining light. That light shone upon a screen in the distance. They called the device 'a projector.' There we saw part of what those folks were calling 'a motion picture film.' In that film, we witnessed people sometimes speaking our language and more often than not, speaking other languages. During a brief intermission, I asked Norman what languages the people were speaking. He said, 'Mostly Russian, with a little Greek and Armenian mixed in.' I thanked him for filling us in on those details.

"At some stage of that film, two soldiers and three civilians, facing a grim situation, passed around a small, hand-held metal device. Each, in turn, would squeeze a lever with their right index finger while pointing the barrel of it at their head. Some pointed it toward their right temples, some pointed it into their mouths. Yet they did this one after another. Also, once in a while, one of them would spin a cylinder inside the metal device, randomizing something about how its contents would line up. After about five times of people doing this, it arrived in the hands of a female civilian who was among them.

"She aimed it at her chest with her left hand and pressed the lever with that hand's index finger. Again, nothing seemed to happen except a light clicking sound. The people in the film kept laughing and drinking and taking turns.

"Someone paused the film. Our main host, the elderly guy we met in the forest, finally revealed that the device is called a 'revolver' and its lever is called a 'trigger.' Someone resumed rolling the film.

"One of the men then pointed the revolver right at his groin and pulled the trigger.

"It did not seem to do anything. The group laughed uproariously, and the other three guys in the group started giving him high fives and congratulating him. The lady blushed. All of a sudden, two ladies who entered the scene and initiated foreplay with the guy who'd just finished taking his turn in that game.

"That guy handed the revolver to another guy, a man who was taking his third turn in this game. That other guy pointed the gun right at his own right temple with his right hand, then squeezed.

"We heard a loud bang. Oh God, the humanity, *that guy's head partially broke apart, and there was blood all over the place. The females in the film were screaming. The men were wailing.* The last person who pulled the trigger *lay motionless on the ground,* with *his head broken open and bleeding profusely.*

"The film soon ended. Norman let us know that this was a secret military training video, and that he had the authorization to show it to us because we were four women of unknown origins speaking a subdialect of Greek and wandering around a mysterious area of Cambodia not far from Angkor Wat, and that it would serve his intelligence gathering operation to *really get to know us better.* He asked what we knew about Russia, China, Vietnam, Laos, and Cambodia.

"We answered truthfully, attesting to the fact that we had no idea that those were even the names of places, though those names did sound familiar: Those place names sounded similar to the entity names of some of the transcendentals, many of whom we at times attempt to attune with via the chanting of mantras and the wielding of iron.

"Sergeant Norman Petty was taken aback at our answer. He decided he better record a brief interview with us on tape. He asked one question after another about how we met him, why we met him, what we knew about this, what we knew about that. The interview went on and on.

"At some stage, he asked what year we thought it was, what calendar we normally use, and other such questions about measuring time.

"At times he looked at his fellow soldiers in sheer disbelief, and they looked the same way right back toward him. On several occasions, quite literally, their jaws dropped.

"They clearly had super-advanced technology, but much of what we had to say seemed earth-shattering to them.

"When it was our turn to ask questions, at some point I asked Norman, 'What's the name of that very dangerous game that we saw those blokes playing with that thing you call a 'revolver?' He answered, 'Russian roulette.'

"I asked him to explain the word 'roulette.' He said, 'You really don't know, do you?' I said, 'Yes, I positively, totally clearly confirm that I do not know what roulette is. What is it?'

"He said something like, 'Imagine a gambling place. Some people there are gathered around a huge spinning wheel. Hmm… Better yet, I'll see if you could stay a little while longer before we try to send you back from whence you came. Would that you be fine with that?'

"I said something like, 'Yes, I believe we can stay as long as it takes to appease the transcendentals, and for my sisters and me to have a good chance of going wherever we should go, whether that would be to 'from whence we came' or somewhere else entirely.'

"He said, 'You're priceless. I don't know if you're on an acid trip or what, but I've got the distinct feeling that you're the real deal, not tripping at all in terms of LSD or what-have-you, but literally time-traveling through our reality in an ultra-mysterious way.'

"Brenda, just looking at you, I can tell that you consent with staying a while longer. Well… What about you and you, Karyellenyia and Suellena?' Those remaining two took turns affirming their consent to stay a while longer.

"Sgt. Petty walked out of the room while two men stood guard silently. I looked at my sisters, and we had devious thoughts of possible attempts at seduction, yet felt that something about aggressive flirtation just didn't seem right for the situation. We did mildly flirt via the motions of our eyes and the ways we smiled at those guards. The two guards stood totally impassive, all business and no pleasure.

"When Sgt. Petty returned, we watched another video. 'Video' is another way to call motion picture films and other things that present motion video displays. That can be of stuff that actually happened or stuff that's an illusion of things that look like they happened, a very sophisticated legerdemain.

"He prefaced that next video by saying that it contained actual footage from a gambling casino. Soon we watched people gathered around a horizontally-oriented wheel that would spin while a small ball would bounce around. The ball would eventually settle into a slot with a specific number. Half of the numbered slots had black, and the other half had red.

"People would gain or lose small coin-like objects called chips, depending on what they wagered in comparison with what the wheel and ball resulted in. He explained that the game is called roulette and that it features a roulette wheel. He stopped the video.

"After that, he took out an empty revolver, something that he called a Colt '45. He demonstrated the way of spinning around the thing in it that could hold multiple instances of things he called bullets.

"There was a silent pause in the room for a while. Then he said, *'Earlier you saw actual footage of people playing Russian roulette. In a place called Russia,* people at some point *invented a game in which the participants* do something *similar to the casino game of roulette,* but instead of winnig or losing chips, *they randomly set up whether they wind up killing themselves or not.'"*

There was silence between them for an extended amount of time. Pattyla could tell that Petrus had been listening closely and that several of his most heavily-relied-upon paradigms had either incinerated or disintegrated (if not permanently, then at least temporarily).

Petrus' cognition had largely turned to stone. Pattyla took him by the hand, looked him in the eyes, and initiated a slow, gentle kiss. His cognition snapped out of the semi-catatonic state, and he started to fully engage in the romance again. Soon, they escalated physicality further.

About an hour later they returned to speaking words at regular levels of audibility.

Petrus said, "You know what, I've changed my mind. I'll decline to go on the trip to that big spiritual-sexual extravaganza after all."

Pattyla said, "Great!"

Elsewhere, there were 65 other cases of men and women among the Dorians considering whether to go to that big shindig. 38 of them, consisting of 24 upper-middle-class-to-upper-class men and 14 women of similar social stature, chose to take that journey.

Meanwhile, the Hebrews and Remians who had considered going to the event eventually, without exception, chose to decline to go. In portions of Northern and Central Europe, 78 Teutons decided that they would go to the big spiritual-sexual festival. They consisted of 34 couples and ten singles.

The event started auspiciously enough, it would seem. However, as the Mycenaeans, Teutons, and Dorians shared many - though not all - of their secrets with one another, and many engaged in highly promiscuous and adventurous sex, things took a turn to the gruesome.

A wealthy Mycenaean benefactor host and his wife were involved with a swap of partners with a wealthy and influential Dorian couple. There was alcohol involved, and there were multiple religious and scientific methods involved. Both temporary couples suddenly found themselves quite literally stuck. The pairings encountered a penis captivus situation. For those not familiar with this terminology, this is when the state of muscles and other flesh in the vagina and the penis during sexual intercourse reach a situation in which, involuntarily for both partners, neither the male nor the female is capable of withdrawing the male member from inside the female chamber.

At first they found this amusing - thrilling even - yet after a while they knew this was starting to jeopardize their health. As the situation lingered, as extra pain and soreness set in, none of the four principal players consented to the traps that their bodies were involuntarily engaged in.

Both men and both women did just about everything within reason that they could to get the situation to work out. Witch doctors and other assistants were called in. Many people tried to help, but over the course of a five-and-a-half-hour ordeal for the female Dorian aristocrat swung into the embrace of the male Mycenaean aristocrat, the female Dorian suffered only moderate genital damage, fully healed in less than a week, whereas the male Mycenaean whose wiener had been trapped for so long suffered such catastrophic connective-tissue damage that his penis was almost dead by a few days later.

Doctors deemed that there was gangrene and recommended for him to consent to letting Dr. Lorena Mussolini perform an emergency penectomy on him. However, he called on Mycenaen deities to help heal the member, and it soon miraculously recovered. With mixed feelings, the witch doctor Lorena congratulated him on his recovery.

That witch doctor's husband, Attorney Wayne Mussolini, had a fun, playful, painful, exotic, and pleasurable night with his wife behind closed doors that night.

Back to the male swinger aristocratic host: several elements of the way he called on those deities to help heal his flesh involved him projecting a mixture of love and hatred toward the sexual partner whose body had recently involuntarily placed his phallus into such precariousness.

He subsequently demanded an apology from the Dorian lady with whom he had just nine days earlier experienced some of the most exhilarating and terrifying moments in his life, and she absolutely refused.

She said to him, in person, "I truly believe that we did nothing wrong. The beings beyond our human control forced upon us a strange and unrelenting challenge.

We survived it, some of our most priceless of organs have experienced injury and recovery, and life goes on. We should remember this with love, with neither apologies nor forgiveness necessary."

He said, "Even though your body was not doing what you intended, something about your heart and mind had something to do with why you body did what it did. And your deities might have been even more responsible for the problem than you were. You bear some responsibility for if your deities possess your body and dare to place such a high-level Mycenaean man into such excessive jeopardy."

She said, "Come on. If you're going to bring transcendentals into the picture, then why do you not consider that it's something to do both with your Mycenaean relations with them and my Dorian relations with them that caused what happened? We could blame both sides and argue all day, but if we trust and love the realities and reality, we really don't have to take a blame-based approach to this whole matter."

He said, "You believe what you choose to believe at this time, but this could have major long-term repercussions."

She said, "You believe what you choose to believe at this time, but this most assuredly will lead to long-term repercussions."

They proceeded with additional pleasantries, eventually agreeing to discuss things further via representatives from a distance in the near future, in hopes of deescalating if possible, and escalating if necessary.

Regarding the other temporary swinging couple, they were stuck for *eight straight hours*. The Dorian man and the Mycenaean woman were able, by the end of that, to relax their bodies enough to disengage, yet by then *both* had endured major bruising, many busted capillaries, etc. Nothing quite as serious as what had happened to portions of the Mycenaean lady's husband's nerve-dense connective tissue, mind you, but still serious.

They resorted to various religious and scientific means with which to heal from the ordeal. However, in the aftermath, similar to what had happened between their normal partners (who had themselves, as you may recall, become temporary partners), the well-to-do Mycenaean lady demanded an apology from the well-to-do Dorian man, and the Dorian gentleman refused.

Portions of the conversation were as follows:

She said, "Although we've healed, something about your heart and mind and soul have to be to blame. I demand an apology!"

He said, "I believe no such apology is warranted, either from you to me or from me to you. We were engaged in a scientific and spiritual sexual adventure, we experienced wonders and terrors, and we survived in good health. Even if we had not recovered good health, *or even if one or both of us had died*, then I would *still* be inclined to believe that *no apologies or expressions of forgiveness would have been called for* in this situation. We consented to doing what we did, we accepted the risks to life and limb, and, yes, you and I *knew that we didn't know* exactly where it would all lead."

She said, "But you're *the man*! I'm *the woman*. In that kind of situation, it is supposed to be *your* responsibility to set up the situation right. It is *my* responsibility *after* you set up the situation right to do my best to manage to help things to *continue* to be right. I *believe* that *you* screwed up something or another in a way that *caused my muscles* to involuntarily *lock up* the way that they did. If you had done a better job as a man, then my body would not have involuntarily trapped you for such a long amount of time."

He said, "Come on! *I did everything in my power* to get the situation to go well in a mutually beneficial way. It's mysterious to the both of us why your muscles contracted and locked up the way that they did. *With the involuntary getting stuck situation, I don't believe either of us are really to blame* at all."

She said, "*What of the differences in our beliefs* regarding God and the gods? We call them deities, you call them transcendentals, we tend to pray to them, you tend to chant mantras with which to channel them, and our cultural differences go on and on. I demand an apology, since if you were more like us, then I think the ordeal would not have happened!"

He said, *"That's it, now you've done it!* I refuse to apologize, and furthermore, although I do not know the full extent to which you are attuned to The Ultimate Reality, I am confident in my people's attunement with The Ultimate Reality. My wife and I are going to depart early from this gathering to return to our homeland. Whether or not you and your husband can work things out peacefully with me and my wife, *I feel fine with whether or not this eventually leads to holy war between The Dorians and The Mycenaeans."*

She said, *"Did you just say what I thought I heard you say? Oh my God, I know that you just said what you said!* How shameless! *How dare you say such things!* We have a sophisticated and advanced culture. You have special religious techniques and such, but I *believe* that we Mycenaeans have solved about 99.9% of reality itself. We have a mostly peaceful, loving, and forgiving culture, yet when some more primitive and warlike peoples like yourselves start to fail to show proper deference to us in connection with our special advances in relationship with God, then we may start headintg down the road toward having to put them back in their place, as cultures not nearly as attuned to honoring the Ultimate God."

He responded, "Yes, *so you think* the Ultimate Level of Reality, the 'Ultimate God' as you phrased it, is someone or something that *you* are more closely attuned with than *we* are. *Quite frankly, I myself do not know at this time the full extent to which anyone is fully attuned with The Ultimate. What I do know is that my people, including myself, are very, very attuned with The Ultimate. We are prepared to live and die with honor. We are prepared for holy peace. We are prepared for holy war. Whether any Dorians, any Mycenaeans, both, or neither are still around by the time the dust settles on the consequences of our dispute, I feel fine about doing whatever I can to get this situation to honor all levels of truth about all levels of reality."*

Not long after that, the Dorian contingent of the gathering returned to their homeland. About half of the Teutonic contingent chose to go with the Dorians to visit them, whereas the other half chose to continue with the festivities hosted by the Mycenaeans.

After this incident, the few Mycenaeans living in Dorian-controlled territories found themselves mysteriously getting into more conflicts with their neighbors, merchants, supervisors, co-workers, and underlings. The same started to apply to Dorians living in Mycenaean-controlled territories. Things started to escalate. Differences of religious conceptualizations, social customs, and scientific developments amplified the escalating tensions.

After a while, an eerie calm suddenly set in. Things seemed to be getting better. Some debated: Is this the calm before the storm or a calm transitioning to long-term peace?

Alas, the controversial upper-class Mycenaean swinging couple, who had felt offended by the lack of any apologies from the upper-class Dorian swinging couple, sent out a diplomatic envoy and several assistants to visit and discuss things further. While there, three members of the visiting group, consisting of two women and one man, were taken on a tour of a holy building. It was a temple devoted to the Lord of Calendars.

Visiting Mycenaeans of the names Juanilias, Janietti, and Traliopi heard a Dorian high priest say to them, "It is of the utmost importance while here to be respectful toward the mysteries of the planets, the plants, the animals, and the humans, and, especially, all cycles and all anti-cycles. Failure to do so in ordinary places can have terrible consequences. Failure to pay that respect here can be *immediately* lethal. *Energies here ramp up to infinity and beyond and all the way to the absolute, or very, very, very, very, very-very close thereto.*

"See the metalwork, the woodwork, and the composite tablets? This place channels other dimensions and times.

"We as Dorians, *for reasons not entirely known to ourselves,* seem to regularly slip through gateways into other places, sometimes it seems very clearly in different centuries - and *occasionally even different millennia* - of alternate universes. Also, we have methods of chanting mantras and pressing upon and pushing around metal, including pumping iron, and these methods can make us stronger and more capable of interacting with the transcendentals. Bearing in mind that there are many things I am not at liberty to divulge unto you, do you have any questions?"

Janietti asked, "What about the differences of how we call on the special beings with the special super-zauber? You tend to call them, insofar as they might be beyond the regular realms, The Transcendentals. We tend to call them deities. The Teutons tend to call them gods. All of us, on at least some occasions, make reference to some ultimate version of the greatest of the great… as 'God.' What about this?"

The high priest answered, "There are many manners of semantics and many dangers of sematics. Semantics and sematics are closely related at times, and, at the other extremes, semantics and sematics can be in rare instances totally unrelated."

Juanilias said, "What about the beginning, the very origins of our universe?"

Traliopi jumped in before the high priest might have otherwise begun to answer, questioning, "You probably have some very powerful ideas on that subject, don't you?"

The high priest answered, "I am not at liberty to go into very full detail on that subject with you. That should be reserved for the initiated, vis-à-vis the specialties of this temple and others like it. Suffice it to say, there are many mysteries about how and why our universe started, and there are many means to get some verbal and nonverbal senses of what happened or might have happened."

It proved to be an amicable meeting between the priest and the three visitors.

The visitors went on to meet with the high-class Dorian couple who had engaged with and subsequently disputed with a high-class Mycenaean couple during the aforementioned Dorian-Mycenaean-Teutonic extravaganza hosted by Mycenaeans. The two couples were able to work out their differences without having to issue any apologies after all.

Peace between Mycenaeans and Dorians started to flourish, perhaps better than it ever had before. Years went by.

However, on the island of Crete one day three ships of extraterrestrials landed and interacted with several Dorians and a multitude of Mycenaeans. The extraterrestrials displayed technologies that would have made many Twenty-First Century C.E. human beings' heads spin. To the Dorians and Mycenaeans present it was spellbinding and breathtaking. After the extraterrestrials flew back into the heavens aboard their starships, the people there negotiated who would take home which of the few artifacts the visitors had left behind. Although there were some tough negotiations, they haggled their way through it peaceably.

The artifacts had strange effects on the minds of all who came within fifty-seven-and-a-half feet of them, over and over again. They stimulated human minds, sometimes amplifying clarity, sometimes amplifying insight, and sometimes imparting seemingly random effects.

Although no living humans knew it at the time, the configurations of the Titanium, Mercury, Gold, Tungsten, Platinum, and just a touch of Iridium-192 were designed for super-advanced scientific purposes. There were twelve artifacts left behind: 1) a one-foot-tall nude male human figurine, 2) a ten-inch-tall nude female figurine, 3) a 44-centimeter-long clothed anaconda figurine, 4) a 35-centimeter-long dimetrodon figurine, 5) a 27-centimeter-long edaphosaurus figurine, 6) a gold-plated five-foot-long / five-foot-wide / six-foot-tall representation of Mount Sumeru, 7) a platinum-plated five-foot tall representation of Mount Everest, 8) a ten-centimeter tall representation of an obelisk identical in proportions to what would later be called The Washington Monument, 9) something that people of later ages would often characterize as a crucifix, 10) something that some sentient beings refer to as a vajra sceptre, 11) an object for which narrative words alone could not do justice (see the diagram that follows this list), and 12) an additional artifact.

SUPPLEMENTAL EXHIBIT: An Excerpt from the Blueprints for the Red, Blue, Black, Grey, White, Green, Crimson, and Gold Item from #11 in the list of objects that remained after the Multi-Starship Visitation of Crete:

Rcvcmbnt G Dntn :::::: H ::::: Z :::: J :::::::::::

::::: ::: ::: ::: $\alpha\beta\gamma\lambda\pi\int\Sigma\Sigma A\Psi\Psi\Omega$ IES

YYYY NN MMM $\forall\exists AE\forall$ MMM $\gamma\gamma\gamma\Delta\Sigma\Phi\Psi$ α

Ion Tion Ation Nation Vation Avation Cavation Excavation

----→   <___   ←------ $\alpha\infty$ ИЯ $\infty\alpha$ $\infty\Omega$
________ > ----→

Dual   Nondual   Duel   Nonduel   NOEL LEON Arbitration

   V. RELIGION   XX. MOMENT OF TRUTH
   VII. PURSUIT   XVI. LAW
   VII. DRIVING   XVI. LIGHTNING

$\infty\alpha$ TETRAGRAM MODELS

ИЯ RN

$\infty\Omega$ VOIDNESS MODELS
SYMMETRY ASYMMETRY CHAOS ORDER THE INEFFABLE

The few Dorians present and the many Mycenaeans present worked out that the latter took home items #4, #5, #7, #10, and #11. The former took home the other seven items. Later, the Dorians traded items #1, #3, and #2 to obtain items #4 and #11.

One year later, tensions between the two camps flared up again. The initial flashpoint involved the son of the high priest from the Dorian temple designed to honor The Lord of Calendars. That son, who was of athletic physique, middle-aged, and married, had performed work in a Mycenaean town, where his supervisors assigned him to work on several carpentry projects with a local heavy-set, middle-aged, unmarried woman. From the very outset there were conflicts.

At some stage the woman accused the man of engaging in bestiality with local goats. He vehemently denied the allegations, and, indeed the accusations were false. However, their mutual supervisors considered the woman too dangerous to upset very thoroughly; that is, they considered, as a risk management decision, that failing to give the Lord of Calendars Dorian Temple's high priest's son due process when evaluating accusations from a local woman against him was, in their minds, a better decision than performing a reasonably thorough investigation into the matter, which they feared might cause that local woman to feel scorned by them, her supervisors.

The high priest's son rightly considered himself the victim of slander, libel, religious discrimination, and outright inhumane treatment in general upon being fired without being given opportunity to reasonably defend his reputation before departure. He felt that they should have chosen a process of acknowledgment and investigation into the delicacies of the situation, but they chose to sidestep that and issue him an ultimatum: Go home now or get executed on the spot. He went back to his Dorian homeland and communicated clearly and accurately to many of his people key specifics of what had transpired.

With coordinated scientific and religious practices by the Dorian high priests and priestesses (some of whom were themselves heavy-set, some of whom were light-set, and many of whom were somewhere between svelte and portly), and ample practices by the accused, a remote energy burst led to the accuser, who bore false witness, suddenly dying by spontaneous human combustion.

The Mycenaeans accused the Dorians of causing the death.

The Dorians responded that indeed the accused man, his father, other high priests, and various high priestesses had used mantras and mudras and other means to channel an attempt to unleash divine wrath. They also acknowledged that they did not know for sure to what extent they had directly caused the case of spontaneous human combustion and to what degree The Transcendentals may have directly intervened, somewhat apart from the auspices of human remote instigation of consequences.

Either way, though, they accepted a degree of plausible responsibility, refused to apologize, expressed that it was their duty to retaliate on behalf of honoring the ultimate realities and The Ultimate Reality itself, and expressed that they would intend to do this type of thing to the Mycenaeans again if they were to engage in this type of disrespect again.

The Mycenaeans declared war. The Dorians responded by also declaring war.

The war was very one-sided. In addition to whatever esoteric spritiual-magico-religious advantages that the Dorians may have had from the outset, they had iron weapons, whereas the Mycenaens had bronze weapons.

Choosing limited amounts of analysis of what went wrong with the Mycenaean culture, after having defeated them, the Dorians chose wholesale annihilation of over 95% of it, replacing it with much of what they considered best from both cultures and a few portions of other cultures as well.

However, as several centuries came and went, tales emerged that weaved together elements of what had happened between the extraterrestrial aliens, the Teutons, the Mycenaeans, and the Dorians, with many embellishments, suppressions, and exotic fable components drawn together in short stories and epic poetry.

The high preisthood of the Dorians left only a minute percentage of themselves in the Mediterranean region. Most of them immigrated elsewhere, including to portions of Africa, the Middle East, and the Himalayas.

A few of the most warrior-oriented among them set up secret societies in places that would later be called Norway, Germany, and Finland.

Chapter Six: Another Angle on What Happened 1,907 ½ Years Before the Tunguska Impact

Dimetrio Elba and Zircon Gilroy debated with two Dorian men about the powder-keg situation between Hebrew, Roman, Greek, and other influences on the Mediterranean and Middle East on 12/31/1 B.C.E. The four participants were, of course, dead in the regular sense, yet still very capable of vigorous discussions regarding all beings dead and alive.

In the twinkling of an eye, they and the vast majority of other beings of the beyond vanished from the beyond and all other existence, for a mysterious 1,907 ½ years of not being anywhere, only to reappear from that hiatus at the moment of impact between the comet and the Earth on June 30th, 1908 C.E.

Even after spending eons in the great beyond, then disappearing and reappearing as they did, they still found themselves having no entirely definite answers to the most ultimate of questions from theology and metaphysics. Some intermediate questions they knew answers regarding from experience, yet answers to many of the biggest questions of the big continued to elude them.

Chapter Seven: A Dimetrodon and a Dorian in a Park in the Great Beyond speak with each other about their impressions of the periods from 1907-2003 and 2018-2019

In a realm of space-time transcending a very exact location in the timelines of being exactly here or there, as it was along the boundary between multiple alternate universes, a conversation took place.

The Dimetrodon partaking of the conversation had just exited a timeline from a 2018 version of Earth. The Dorian present had come from a timeline from a July 3rd, 2019 version of Earth.

Rather than discussing many specifics about where they had just been, they briefly took turns sharing impressions about the period from June 30th, 1908 to April 3rd, 2003 and other times.

The quadruped said, "You sure you want to hear me improvise a tale of weaving it together, part fact and part fantasy?"

The biped responded,"Yes, I've witnessed so much strange stuff the past few years, and I know you've witnessed much. Please tell me about your impressions."

"Of all the people and places and things I've encountered," said the quadruped, "at this time the strongest impression I have is that there is a very big 'it' that has to do with the female quadruped being Lorentzia Exiguus and the biped Dionysius Exiguus. I can't fathom exactly what it is about them, but there are so many things peculiar from where I stand: First, although separated by over 250 million years on the normal timelines of their worlds, they share the same surname. Second, somewhere in the beyond, I witnessed them about forty-five feet in front of me, at Stonehenge on the day of the Winter Solstice in 1907 A.D., performing a ceremony, while all but a few of the 'living' present could not see them or me. Three other spies were accompanying me, and we could not make heads or tails about how and why those two were there together at the same time. Therefore, although there are many things I know and many things I do not know about the middle of 1908 to early April in the year 2003, I believe that those two Exiguuses are very much in the nexus of how and why much of the mysterious stuff happened the way it did. What do you think?"

The biped thought for a moment, then stated, "I think you're onto something, but I am not very familiar with either of those two mysterious Exiguuses. By the way, do you know if the contemporary quadrupeds of over 251 million years before Hurricane Dorian, the quadrupeds Lorentzia Dorian and Lorentzia Exiguus have ever met each other?"

The dimetrodon said, "I'm not completely sure, but during some portions of my espionage – portions that I am at liberty to disclose to you – I found evidence that they most likely met each other in the year 1001 AD in Portugal and again in the year 1998 in Tunisia. Why do you ask?"

The human said, "Another piece of the puzzle. Or maybe two more pieces that can have manifold roles in many puzzles."

The quadruped said, "Fair enough. Tell me more about whatever you have on your mind that you would like to share right now."

The Dorian said, "In contrast with your focus on specific pairs of beings, I have noticed some peculiarities about families of the names Mussolini, Einstein, de Leon, Massey, Wilson, and Heath. I don't know way too much about them, but I do know enough to tell that there's some funky it-loads of something going on with them. So much wonderful and terrible stuff from 1907-2003, but maybe we should focus more attention to 2018 and 2019. What do you think about those years in most of the versions of Earth that you are aware of?"

The Dimetrodon answered, "It-loads of stuff: what a beautiful transformation of language. Some beings are so often prone to say, 'God damn it,' yet this occasion, I believe calls for us to say, 'God bless it!'"

The Dorian seconded the motion: "God bless it!"

The Dimetrodon then continued, "The living humans of Earth in every universe I could find seemed to have devolved into a terrible state of affairs by the Northern Hemisphere's Winter Solstice 2018. That was, and in some universes is, a state in which about one-third to two-thirds of the human race have such levels of tribalism and mental distortion, as well as yearnings for easy street, that it's not surprising that *The Planet Mars as a Whole* and *The Planet Jupiter as a Whole* perform a joint biological attack on *The Planet Earth as a Whole* in *September 2019* in virtually *every* possible universe."

Chapter Eight: Flashbacks to Around 65 Million Years Prior to The Modern World, in portions of multiple alternate universes

Part I of the flashbacks and tangents to around 65,000,000 earth-sun orbits before:

In the year 65,895,250 BC, the ghosts and other spiritually-beyond transitional beings of the dimetrodons and other organisms of the pre-Triassic periods of the Earth witnessed as, in the twinkling of an eye, millions of dinosaurs and mammals and other living earthlings achieved super-powerful telepathic attunement with them. Most of this was at a semiconscious level for the living, and most of this was at a conscious level for the dead and semi-dead. Interspecies telepathy among dinosaurs soon ramped up exponentially.

This became especially noticeable on the areas in and near what the humans would later call The Yucatan Peninsula. It was there that a large omnivorous bipedal dinosaur, with a brain small in physical stature compared to the higher-dimensional capabilities it possessed, experienced a revelation. That being was a somewhat hermaphroditic dinosaur, about 68% male and about 32% female. As conventional for some dinosaurs of that time, it did not choose to conceive of itself as having a name, rather it conceived of itself in a manner of, "I am what I am, it is what it is, and ideas like 'I' and 'it' have their own ways of transcending. The energies of presence can be self-evident of who we are, without overt over-structuring."

It gathered with a group of dinosaurs, proto-birds, birds, mammals, and reptiles, who sensed its awesome presence of mind. Welcomed and telepathically invited by the others, it went into an extended telepathic story supplemented with intermittent gestures and vocals. Many of the living, multitudes of the dead, and flocks of semi-dead gathered to listen closely as that hermaphroditic dinosaur presented a fable or a theory.

That sentient being proceeded to state, "We live in something called a universe. This universe is one of many, or perhaps infinitely-analog-style sliding ranges of universes. We can transition from one universe to another, and perhaps many of us do this from time to time, whether we are consciously aware of it or not.

"Although I do not know for sure whether the following is just exactly how we've arrived where we are, nevertheless, I shall present a vision I've had as a hypothesis for the history of our universe from its inception to the present.

"Within a fabric of ambiguous spatiotemporal relations, five primordial beings spontaneously arose from sheer nothingness. They soon induced an intense explosion in which nothingness-&-potential became everythingness-&-all-potentials. Boom!!

"This eventually led to this place we live on, a giant place within many much larger places, themselves within a vastness beyond all conceivability. Long ago, the large orbiter of reflective light, which some have called 'the moon,' orbited a realm in which the first intelligent being was born. The first being was a bird, which the transcendental primordial five beings (who were and are 'super-intelligent beings' rather than merely 'intelligent beings') induced into becoming alive by charming an inanimate stone into becoming animate.

"That stone was somewhere on this planet that we now live on, long before a collision between Proto-Earth and Proto-Moon resulted in Earth and Moon and many changes. That stone hatched from being a stone to being the first bird. Therefore, if we consider the animated stone to qualify as an egg, then the first bird egg came before the first bird; whereas if we consider the animated stone to have been something other than an egg, then the first bird came before the first bird egg. That bird became capable of laying a living egg after the electromagnetics of the suddenly-conscious planet, which in that instance chose to act as a male planet, though it more usually acts as a female planet.

"The first bird, an intelligent-though-not-yet-super-intelligent being, a few years after its hatching from an animate stone, became impregnated by the Earth, during an instance in which that planet we live on chose to act as a male for a while. The bird subsequently laid an egg, which hatched into a male bird. After the first bird cared for that male second bird sufficiently, the Earth chose to act as a female for a while. The planet then engaged in telepathic and psychokinetic sex with the second bird, and the result of this act of transcendental mating was that the Earth was ready to have many independent instances of inanimate matter transitioning directly into animate biological beings of spatiotemporal, conscious, semiconscious, and subconscious energetic statics and dynamics. And Earth, for millions of years, proceeded to generate much life in a feminine mode.

"However, Earth on rare occasions chose to switch to generating life in a masculine mode again. Meanwhile, the extremely-primordial ultra-super-intelligence or ultra-super-intelligences who had already been in existence prior to even the five primordial super-intelligences chose to intervene. He and/or She and/or It and/or They suddenly chose to spontaneously generate the first bipedal two-armed humanoids.

"Yes, I am aware that many of those gathered here today are skeptical that the legendary alleged-to-exist humanoids have ever existed here or anywhere else. We hear such strange stories of the humanoids who sometimes arrive on spaceships, telepathically telling some of us tales of planets and solar systems located in the heavens, and we wonder the dinosaurs and others who speak of encountering them are making this stuff up, yet in this hypothetical vision, at least some of them were around prior to the super-collision between Proto-Earth and Proto-Moon. Life started to flourish. It's a matter of semantics whether we identify Proto-Earth with being an early stage of Earth or something not quite qualifying yet as early Earth, by the way.

"The humanoids also referred to themselves as 'people.' They had a seemingly supernatural way of manipulating most other living, biological, sentient beings of the planet.

"Over time, the peoples and animals and plants developed profound symbiosis. However, some prior version of a being who was in some ways what became me and who in some ways was not at all what became me, a being I sense was a powerful male humanoid, foretold that all humanoids and most non-humanoid sentient beings of the planet would vanish in the flash of an eye just before a planetary total or nearly total extinction event. Soon thereafter, Earth and Moon collided, and although life did not go totally extinct, it was almost total extinction for life there. That resulted in the New Earth and the New Moon. Alternatively, we could say that Proto-Earth and Proto-Moon collided, resulting in Earth and Moon.

"A similar cycle repeated some untold number of times as divine punishment for the inhabitants having gone too far astray. Each time, *The Powers That Be* chose to *manipulate* the fabrics of *All Realities* to make scientific evidence lead humans of a future cycle *lull themselves and others* into *thinking that no such cycles had ever happened* before. *Yet, happen before they did.*

"Eventually, a class of beings that some humans refer to as dimetrodons, kind of esembling what spinosaurs transformed into quadrupeds might look like, did something about this weird cycle of death. Through their development of embedding eleventh-generation wireless means of telecommunication into their very biological systems, they achieved sufficient power to stand toe-to-toe in battle with The Powers That Be, just enough to break our planet free from the earth-moon-collision repetitive death trap. This came at a great cost, though, as within our timeline, the dimetrodons went nearly extinct about 206 million years ago, then went totally extinct relative to worldly life 180 million years ago. That being said, many of the dimetrodons achieved advanced soteriological methodologies prior to their worldly deaths, with which their consciousnesses are in our very presence today as among the transcendental and semi-transcendental retinue of the great beyond.

"I do not know for sure, but I sense that we may be about to go extinct. Whether or not that happens soon, take heed, if we can tap into the cosmic consciousness of the dimetrodons and the primordial beings, we may have hope for something of the beyond."

This speech received celebratory telepathic applause, together with visible and audible foot stomping and jumping for joy. In the distance, looking up to the heavens, though, they soon saw it rapidly approaching in the upper atmosphere.

An asteroid hit Earth in the very region of that gathering, generating a Richter-13-magnitude quake and other mass-extinction-inducing consequences.

....

....

Part II of select flashbacks and tangents to around 65,000,000 earth-sun orbits prior to the emergence of the modern world:

The 68%-male/32%-female dinosaur who completed an ode to speculative cosmology, together with all of its entourage, died instantly when the KpG asteroid hit Earth in the very area in which they had been reveling. For about 2,000 years, "they" were in many respects totally gone from all of reality, neither of consciousness nor of any definite physical presence or extensionality of this or any other realm.

After those years had gone by, about 5% of them re-manifested in the great beyond in the very presence of the transcendent beings Dimetrio Elba and Zircon Gilroy, who had by that time resolved their over-200-million-year feud. Remember that their dispute with each other started long before either had passed on from the state of the living, and that it was one of the main drivers of the dozens upon dozens of millions of years of what some would call synapsids-versus-reptiles holy war.

With the uber-catastrophic celestial impact event and all that went with it, the reptiles and synapsids of *both* the here-and-now *and* the beyond had set aside their clingings to real or perceived grievances against each other, and the holy war gave way to a long period of holy peace.

Zircon and Elba chose to speak with the 68%M/32%F visionary while in an assembly of spirits, transcendental beings, and others. Zircon said, "Although you currently consider yourself to be nameless and transcending gender, it would be more convenient at this time for us to grant some way of categorizing you, at least for some forms of conceptualization. Of course, as with your inner thoughts, in many ways you are who and what you are, beyond the limits of conceptual over-structuralism, even as we grant you what we will.

"My name is Zircon, and, as you have probably surmised by now, with my arguably-rather-ostentatious demonstration of shape-shifting while speaking, I am a shape-shifter. That being said, at some core levels of identity, I am a highly-advanced reptile, which means in some ways I am a closer relative to you than the synapsids, though in other ways the synapsids are closer relatives to you. I shall now hand center stage speaking over to Doctor Elba."

Dimetrio Elba, whom various beings of the beyond had granted the title "Doctor," started to speak, amidst an assembly that had grown essentially absolute in its silence and attentiveness. "I am Dr. Dimetrio Elba, and I was a dimetrodon prior to my death and transition into the bardo realm. Rather than reincarnating or becoming a strength-challenged hungry ghost, I transitioned with my memory intact into some quasi-transcendental states of being. Similarly, my friend Zircon, who for over 200 million years had been an enemy of mine, and, at the times of our worldly deaths we had still been in a relationship of enmity; he transitioned from being a shapeshifting reptile of indeterminate species into also becoming a memory-intact quasi-transcendental being. Each of us often held high ranks on the respective sides of epic warfare, often telepathically using unsuspecting living dinosaurs, birds, and insects as unknowingly-manipulated proxy warriors.

"As you made your grand speech just before dying, there was much in it that we knew to be true, much that we knew to be false yet indirectly-truthful if taken as a fable, and much of it that was fundamentally unknown to us with respect to how-true-or-how-false. You've been somewhere in the deep beyond, we know not exactly where or how, but you've suddenly appeared a little while ago with us in the beyond. For quite a while, in anticipation that this day might come, Zircon and I debated whether to grant you a name, and if so, then what. We eventually negotiated our way into an agreement."

Elba then looked Zircon in the eye and nodded. The both of them then looked over at the 68%M/32%F visionary and said in unison, "We christen you 'Christopher Morphy Exiguus,' and we declare you, for general purposes, to be considered a male."

Christopher Exiguus stood silently for a few seconds, then replied, "I respect what has transpired here today. Thank you for granting these alternate conceptualizations and communication devices to me."

Elba and Zircon said, almost-though-not-entirely-in-unison, "You're welcome."

Dimetrio Elba continued, "I believe it best now that three sisters and two brothers from the previous mass extinction event on Earth take turns chiming in with their hypotheses on the origins of the realities that led to our present reality. First up, Susannah Oberstein. Please enlighten us, s'il vous plaît."

Susannah chimed in, "Guten Tag! Although the full truth values and falsehood values of the following are largely unknown, here goes another theoretical vision on the origins of the realities.

"In the beginning all universes and multiverses already quasi-existed within a quantum uncertainty probability wave of potential. That was within the fabric of absolute nothingness, yet this was not a stable way for things to permanently remain. The potentialities gave way to actualities. Ever since, beings have come and gone, incarnated and refrained from incarnating, reincarnated and refrained from reincarnating, and changed in almost limitless ways.

"Here we are now, but each of us were also, at least a trace of us, there... way back there... at the dawn of creation itself." She looked to Elba and nodded.

Elba spoke thusly, "Next, a dialogue between Pandora Brooks and Pandara Smithsonian."

Brooks gently whispered, "Time." Few noticed as she did that.

She then spoke in a normal voice. "I am one of the beings of the name Pandora. The being currently immediately to my left is one of the beings of the name

Pandara. Her surname is Smithsonian, and my surname is Brooks. I hypothesize that Christopher Exiguus was correct when he, prior to departing normal life to enter the great beyond and before receiving his name, hypothesized that eons earlier a huge amount of that which is him had manifested as a powerful humanoid. What do you think of this, Smithsonian?"

Pandara Smithsonian answered, "I am rather skeptical of that hypothesis. It may be difficult or impossible to ascertain whether it is true, and the overall pattern strikes me as rather far-fetched. However, let's turn our attention, if we may, to what I found most shocking about the mysterious speech that preceded the catastrophe.

"He, who back then was considered one of the many Its-With-No-Name, theorized that there have been many cycles in which Earth-or-Proto-Earth collides with Moon-or-Proto-Moon, resulting in New-Earth-or-Earth and New-Moon-or-Moon. Even more bizarre, his theory claimed that 'The Powers That Be' would somehow manipulate *all* of the space and time to lull the eventually-reemerging human scientists into thinking it was the first time around for the humans. Then those Powers would sit back and watch whether humanity and the other earthlings would screw things up royally all over again, judge in the affirmative, manipulate the Moon out of orbit to have it collide with Earth, generate a tragic impact of unspeakable proportions, wipe out all or nearly all life on Earth, then set up a new cycle. Reading between the lines, part of that would involve having the evidence of past advanced civilizations, *or perhaps nearly all the evidence of past advanced civilizations*, vanish into thin air (or some similar process of concealment). These make my mind spin with bewilderment!! Sister Brooks, what do you think?"

Brooks delved into the issues somewhat differently, "What about it? It seems very plausible to me. Dimetrodon, edaphosaurian, reptilian, and human legends often concur with each other on the notion of a grand cosmic cycle, in which the more-temporal-and-less-transcendent beings do what they do, sometimes for better, sometimes for the worse, then face the judgment of The Absolute. Although they disagree on many points, the big picture tends to look very much that way. It seems entirely possible that The Absolute might, via all intermediaries, instigate one of the mechanisms of a series of judgment days to include the Moon colliding into the Earth.

Now, letting go of those esoteric depths of antiquity, and returning focus to the here and now, Earth is currently in a mass extinction event that started 2,000 years ago with that Yucatan impact. That marked the approximate end of the Cretaceous period, and it could be an example of how The Powers That Be don't have to go to the utter extremity of causing an Earth-Moon collision to deliver mass casualties."

Smithsonian and Brooks looked at each other and the rest of assembly in silence. After a little while, Zircon spoke up. "Next, let's have the male druid humanoid Abram Cadavarious materialize before us and speak, if he dares to do so. If not, then we'll turn to a backup speaker.

"Mr. Cadavarious, whether you currently consider yourself primarily a Christian, Hindu, Buddhist, Druid, or something else, and whatever universe and dimension you currently reside in, we humbly request that you find the higher-dimensional space-time to let your presence be known.

Abram Cadavarious indeed immediately materialized before them, teleporting from somewhere unknown to the assembly. "Here I am, just arriving from an alternate universe that finds itself at the beginning of Hurricane Season in a year known there as 2019 Anno Domini or 2019 Common Era among a very high percentage of the living humans. The meteorological authorities there, in their infinite wisdom, chose to name the upcoming fourth storm of the Atlantic Hurricane Season 'Dorian.' It seems perfectly fortuitous that you called on me to come over, because just prior to that I was thinking of coming here, whether invited or not. While I was mulling that possibility, to go or not to go, *you suddenly invited me and I felt it*. Already a being somewhat of the beyond, *your calling me and my thinking* about arriving *were sufficient* to teleport me here via *higher-dimensional folded space-time* of many dimensions and *many intertwined universes*.

"That universe I came from also had a cataclysmic impact about 65 million years before the so-called common era, also resulting in a mass extinction. That being said, being able to take in the really big picture, a view coordinating eons and galaxies and hyperspace, the humans of that universe I was in might be on the brink of instigating a new mass extinction, *with a Martian microbe that teleported itself into their presence* being just one of myriads of instruments of death. The Martian microbe I spoke of is something of a master microbe, and it's capable of subtly remotely influencing other biological agents into generating pandemics.

"Their karma, whether anyone refers to it as beings reaping what they sow or causation or the way things go, is inviting to their world an armada of annihilations.

"I do not know who has the more brutal path forward, you or them. I do know that in some future scenarios, your very universe could lead to either their very universe or something extremely similar. Best wishes with choosing wisely.

"How do you believe I could best be of help to you?"

Dr. Elba answered, "I belive you have already helped immensely with the insights that you have just provided. The next way you could help best, I believe, would be to stay a while longer, listen to the next speaker, then decide what *you* believe best *after* receiving that *additional* information. Are you ready?"

Mr. Cadavarious said, "Yes. Let's go for it!"

Next came from Dr. Elba the utterance, "I turn the floor over to one of *my* primary *trainers* from the days of my youth, a dimetrodon who was wise and powerful *long* before I started to approach his stature. Without further ado, here's Enochus Gilroy Rubicon Geddinger."

Enochus Geddinger began yet another phase of this meeting by saying, "Mr. Cadavarious and I rarely share physical presence at a venue. This is ultra-rare, much like the spontaneous, sometimes-allegedly-supernatural occurrence of the element Technetium."

"Seven, Ten, Eighteen, Thirty-Eight, Twenty-Seven, Forty-Eight, Fifty-Five,

Eighty-Seven. In accordance with prophecy, that KpG asteroid impact happened. If I understand the next part of the prophecies and how they relate to reality properly, the mammals will rise in stature, and one day human beings, a special class of humanoids, will be prolific wielders of advanced mechanical technologies. They will also have major mixtures of compassion, passion, dispassion, wisdom, folly, hatred, apathy, love, agitation, and equanimity. They will be like nothing the planet has ever seen before."

"That is, unless maybe if that crazy or maybe-not-so-crazy theory about repetitive earth-moon-collisions-cum-vanishing-of-tech-evidence cycles is correct. On the other hand, if Abram Cadavarious is correct about travel between different times from different universes, then the very notions of 'before' and 'after' are sometimes-illusory parts of a cosmic labyrinth of epic proportions."

Chapter Nine: The September 23rd-29th, 2019 Convergence

As meteoroligists and others learned about the names declared to go with the storms of the 2019 Atlantic Hurricane Season, it drew many laughs from lots of folks.

People in Jamaica and nearby areas did not find it quite so funny when Hurricane Dorian came a-calling and went on a rampage. Elsewhere, in strategic locations of the great beyond, still never having fully resolved the religious differences between the believers among them in nondenominational spiritualism, Sikhism, Judaism, Christianity, Islam, Buddhism, Jainism, agnosticism, and other things, a coalition including Dimetrodons, Plesiosaurs, Hebrew humans, Gentile humans, Dorians, Ionians, Druids, and others gathered for a serious convention.

After much deliberation, they decided that September 23rd, 2019 would be the perfect day to call on all Ponderosa pine trees on Earth and all the spirits of the Petrified Forest of the American desert southwest to make it happen: The opening of all Pandora's boxes, all Pandara's boxes, and the full brunt of all paranormal activities. However, an unexpected guest materialized from nowhere.

The version of Gary Mark Gilmore who in one of the most exotic of universes rose from common criminal to becoming the 40th President of the United States, even receiving an endorsement from Governor Reagan (President Ronald Reagan before he became the 41st President of the United States of America relative to that universe) on his way to replacing President Jimmy Carter in that role, said, "Stop! The time is not quite right. You should wait."

A Hasidic Jew and a Vajrayana Buddhist seated beside each other about forty-two yards away from GMG were seated behind an MGM executive who had been shot to death by a time traveler who targeted him.

The three of them looked at each other in a mixture of belief, disbelief, and amazement at what they just witnessed. The former MGM executive, who was in some ways still a Metro-Goldwyn-Mayer executive on account of how some of his duties in the beyond involved influencing his former employer in attempts to steer reality toward the good, the better, and the best in the long run, spoke up. "Which version of Gary Mark Gilmore are you? Please, give an elevator speech bio."

GMG responded, "After early years of crime, I cleaned up my act. Then with the help of some influential families, I became an attorney. From law I rose to politics. In politics I made it to the top, with a combination of fearlessness and tenacity. We even achieved world peace for about ten months in my universe in the year 2010, long after I had left office. Then Earth got into the cross hairs of an interstellar war between extraterrestrial aliens. Early in 2012, well, actually, late in the first half of that year, June 10th to be precise, a nuclear bomb vaporized a bunch of people, including myself. I wandered from one universe to another, met up with twenty-six different versions of myself, and have helped some of the beings here and there to find their way through the winding and forking paths of the many multi-verses."

The former movie executive was not impressed. "I am not so concerned about whether or not your life was as glorious as you portrayed it, but I am skeptical about why we should trust you to know better than our consensus in this gathering. Give us something to consider about why we should delay the unleashing of the full brunt of the paranormal to the best of our abilities so help us God."

Gary Gilmore said, "In some ways it's funny that you mentioned that, because, based on my past experiences in the great beyond, you will almost definitely you yourselves split into multiple realities in which different versions do different things, some taking my suggestion, some rejecting it, and some finding some third or fourth alternative as the way to go."

Sure enough, the very reality within that convention split into multiple realities in which some versions unleashed the full brunt of the paranormal, some released limited magnitudes of it, and some showed restraint until the year 2021.

Many of the versions who did indeed open those Pandora's boxes and Pandara's boxes in the third quarter of 2019 chose to have the openings occur to coincide with the period of September 23rd to 29th that year.

Chapter Ten: 2021, Ponderosa Pines, Pandara's Boxes, Pandora's Boxes, 2022, and the Return of the Eurypterids

"This is totally unconscionable, that dude, Chief Justice John Roberts basically took a torch to Article II of the Constitution," said Sammy Watts to his relative Geronimo Watts.

"Yeah, I think that's just what happened. It's been all over talk radio. I don't know just what will happen six days from now, but I hope it really shakes people up in what we have left of this republic," replied Geronimo.

Elsewhere, their ex-wives, Cheryl Nobel and Shirley Watts were having tea and espresso in a coffee shop. Ms. Nobel said, "Thank goodness that goodness prevailed!"

Ms. Watts replied, "Yeah, there's too much toxic masculinity in this country. I think things are about to get better. We just need to get past the controversies expected on January 6th, then things will be back to being kind of normal. Does your ex Sammy still bother you lately?"

Cheryl Nobel said, "No, I think he knows better, especially since the time when my new husband gave him a serious tongue lashing after he showed up at our door at 10:30 PM, drunk and stuttering about how he loves me and that he was wrong and all that desperate clinging he has to the way things used to be."

Shirley said, "Yeah, well good riddance! I'm very happy for you."

Ms. Nobel and Ms. Watts were in Portland, Oregon, whereas Sammy and Geronimo Watts were in Stafford, Texas. Back in Stafford, Geronimo asked, "So, when was the last time you spoke with you know who?"

Sammy said, "Oh, you just had to bring that up? Well, it was about two years ago. I was drinking, and I drove over to her house, where she and her new hubbie, Giancarlo Ordaz, were living in a mansion. Maybe it was not the best decision I've ever made. Well, Giancarlo did not hit me or even make physical contact, but he did pull me aside to say, 'Bro, it's over. She and I are happily married and we are probably going to stay that way as long as we're both still alive. But I have some great news, brother!'" He paused, giving Geronimo a chance to inquire further or to change to another subject.

Geronimo said, "Well, what was the 'great news' that he had to share with you?"

Sammy explained, "He said, 'I've got this groovy Freddy Fender CD, and I'd like to give it to you for you to listen to. If you don't like it, just give it back and I'll accept it. But if you do like it, go ahead and keep it, maybe it'll help you accept that she currently wants to be with me, not you, but we don't know for sure if things will always be this way. After all, stranger shit's happened in the history of this crazy planet!"

Geronimo asked, "Do you remember more exactly when it was that he gave you that Freddy Fender CD?"

Sammy said, "Hmm, let me try to put this together. Oh, I've got it. I don't remember the exact date as a month and year, but I remember clearly that it was when Tropical Storm Imelda was making headlines."

Geronimo's eyes opened wide and his pupils dilated. "No shit?! That seems like almost a lifetime ago, after all that COVID stuff went down earlier this year, then all this election weirdness went down recently... and is still going on."

Sammy chimed in again, "Just six days to go until a bunch of those folks gather at the capitol. I hope they really rock those dirty Democrats!"

Geronimo said, "Yeah, so do I. It's not like they're expecting to do something totally illegal, like storm the capitol, right?"

Sammy said, "Right on, right on! Country still seems headed to hell, but maybe with a little hell-raising in protest of a stolen election, yeah, yeah baby, yeah, give 'em hell. Give 'em hell!"

Back in Portland, Shirley and Cheryl had moved on to talk about the environment. Shirley asked, "Maybe the COVID-19 was a way for Mother Earth to tell everyone, pay attention, protect the environment, don't use so many fossil fuels, ya think?"

Cheryl said, "Yeah, I mean who are we as humans to mess with the environment? Of course, I wouldn't be surprised if the Earth itself intentionally made the entire Covid crisis stuff happen, and then some of the government types ended up blaming each other. Trump blamed people, Biden blamed people, the Chinese blamed America, many Americans blamed China, but maybe it was the Earth itself that made this happen."

Observing both New Year's Eve conversations from near the end of the Year 2020, via monitors in the beyond, Zircon and Dimetrio looked at each other and knew what each other were thinking: It was not the Earth that instigated Covid-19 getting unleashed unto the world, it was a strategem from the entirety of Planet Mars and the entirety of Planet Jupiter, as conscious holistic planet entities, to retaliate against earthlings on behalf of earthlings and all other beings.

The backdrop of their strategy was too many people causing too much trouble across the entire solar system with the distortions of their mindsets and lifestyles, spanning the entire political spectrum and the entire socioeconomic spectrum. Therefore, those planets manipulated the choices of millions in order to influence humans, microbes, and other agents to, from August 2019 onward, go on a path leading directly to the 2020 large-scale lockdowns across much of the civilized world. The alchemy not of transmutation of base metals into gold, but of the transmutation of microbes and rearrangements to grant them access to plenty of human hosts.

In Houston, TX, a young man named Josh started to cough about the time that Tropical Storm Imelda reached its zenith of activity in September 2019. He had contracted a Martian microbe, which had slipped through a shortcut in the fabric of space-time to go directly from Mars to Earth. That microbe had special abilities, despite its lack of what scientists would typically call 'a brain,' to remotely influence other microbes and the humans in closest contact with them to act in a more pro-microbe manner. At some stage, it was one of the many factors contributing to the spread of illnesses.

Technically, though few of the inter-universal time-travelers knew it, the involvement of Jupiter and Mars in the spread of Covid-19 was only true over some ranges of universes. There were also ranges of universes in which the consciousnesses of those two planets refrained from instigating the 2020 Covid-19 craziness on Earth, yet the 2020 Covid-19 craziness on Earth still reared its head anyway. Only in some exceptional cases of universes did that planet somehow avoid that mayhem.

In one of the universes in which the coalition of many beings in the beyond who had a sudden visit from the ghost of U.S. President Gary Gilmore of an alternate reality, those beings chose to hold off on the main opening of Pandora's boxes and Pandara's boxes until Friday, December 3rd, 2021.

They gathered together at 2 AM Central Time in downtown Houston, then, invisibly to most living creatures on Earth, walked toward the hospital district. In that district, they then telepathically linked minds with a gathering of similar beings in Fresno, California, then opened a telepathic link to all Ponderosa pine trees living on the planet. Soon, gathering the mental powers of quintillions of beings, and with full faith that the time was right for it, they fully opened the floodgates to the full brunt of the paranormal.

Noon on August 23rd, 2022, 40 nautical miles from the east coast of Japan, fishermen lifted their nets from the depths of the ocean. Shocked to see a sea creature that looked like a ten-foot long scorpion, they arranged for scientists to haul off the creature. In a secret underwater government facility off the coast of Japan, cryptozoologists, paleontologists, and others from several Asian countries gathered and analyzed the specimen.

Japanese high-ranking military biologist Dr. Yamamoto called his American counterpart Dr. Sagovia to say, "Remember how earlier this month you shared footage of how your team acquired a living Eurypterid? Well, we've acquired a living one ourselves, only this one seems to be a twelve-foot long *Jaekelopterus rhenaniae*."

Dr. Sagovia exclaimed, "And I thought the one we caught was huge! The official fossil records showed eight feet as the most likely limit from way back when, and our nine-foot specimen was quite a shocker. And now a twelve-footer from a part of the Pacific almost half a world away from where we found ours. The Eurypterids are back. God help us all!"

Epilogue: Nonfiction Postscripts I & II

A Nonfiction Postscript I: When I walked along Westheimer and nearby areas in something like August 2021 and first met Andrew Dane Mireles, at some stage within the long conversation there was an informative exchange very much like this:

ADM: In early 2020 something strange happened.

MJB: What did you experience?

ADM: I experienced January 1st that year. Then things went on some loops, something like from January 1st to January 2nd back to the 1st. Then January 2nd again, then to the 3rd, then back to New Year's Day, then to the second... After a long time, I was finally able to reach January 4th that year.

MJB: It's very interesting that you said that, because I experienced something similar on September 27th, 2019. Specifically, I went to bed at something like 8:30 or 9:30 PM, a while after the sun had fully gone down that day. Time went by. Suddenly, in the facility where I was at, a man woke me up from bed; he also woke up many other people there. He said in a loud and commanding voice, "Everybody out of bed. WE ARE OUT OF TIME."
   A group of us gathered in a room with a television set, yet the TV was off.
   Soon, one of the people leading the meeting asked me, as part of the brief group discussion, something like, "Hey, Cul De Sac, what do you think President Trump just did?" I said, "Declared martial law."
   I then shut up for most or all of the remainder and listened to what other folks said, yet there did not seem to be any clear statement from anybody as to whether the strange hypothesis I presented in this very bizarre setting was spot-on or not.
   Soon, almost everyone to go back to bed. I went back to sleep.
   When I next woke up, I noticed that there was plenty of light outside and that the television showed clearly that it was early evening, *something like 6:20 PM* and that *the date was* still *September 27th, 2019.*
   The main thing I noticed on the local Houston evening news was that a prominent local police officer had been shot and killed.

A Nonfiction Postscript II: Let one of the roles of this epilogue be to serve as a supplemental memorial to Science Fiction Author Harlan Ellison and to Harris County Deputy Sheriff Sandeep Singh Dhaliwal, neither of whom I met in this lifetime prior to their earthly deaths, yet in whose honor I am choosing to mention this.

Deputy Sheriff Dhaliwal was, indeed, the officer described on TV in the early-evening news story, which I did not experience during the first time around, but which I did experience during the second time around. In response to how some might contend that hardly anyone other than Andrew and I would believe in the legitimacy of these experiences, I will mention three things:

1) The experience I had of going from post-dusk 9/27/2019 back to pre-sunset 9/27/2019 was of the class of experiences of certainty in my memory, and the vital observations were clearly from waking life rather than a dream state.

2) A strange elderly man who said he had served in Vietnam, later changed from being a U.S. citizen to becoming a citizen of Spain, and said his name was Billy walked into a bar and grill where I was dining in the evening of St. Brigid's Day 2022, in Austin, Texas, and after he made many outlandish claims about things he had experienced, at some point in that evening I told him, not about my 9/27/2019 perhaps inexplicable experience but about Andrew Mireles's seemingly inexplicable experience from the first few days of 2020. That Billy and I agreed that the Mireles tale of early 2020 time loops seemed plausible, given that both he and I had experienced things of similar orders of magnitude of weirdness to what Andrew told of experiencing.

3) I witnessed an Internet story that reported that Texas A&M had lost to Colorado in college football early in the 2021 NCAA season, then witnessed reports that Texas A&M had defeated Colorado in the very same game that the prior Internet story described, in rather dramatic terms, that Texas A&M had been defeated. When the game actually happened, I was oblivious to it happening and did not catch any of it live on TV, as far as I recall. As time went by, I occasionally asked a few people about this, and at least one person corroborated having experienced a Mandela effect with that game. The corroborating man at some stage made a passing remark like, "Oh, that's the game that they played twice."

About the Author and Various Other Beings

(A chronicle which shall at times transition back and forth between modes of third person voice and first person voice)

Part I: A list of names, declining to specify which, of whom and to whom, this might best refer, in each case of a name or a combination of names:

Samantabhadra

The Gregorian Calendar

The Tibetan Calendar

Katherine Navarette

Fannin

Eva-Maria Gortner

Stephen Zeff

Rice University

Lyle Boudreaux

Heather Flores

J.M. Hanks High School

Duke University

The University of Texas at Austin

The University of Michigan

Baylor University

Adibuddha

Trinity

Unity

Multiplicity

Vajrasattva

Part II

Insofar as this is within a somewhat-observable lifetime, relative to various reference frames of space-time, etc., the author of this book has resided in East Asia, New Hampshire, Montana, Texas, and North Carolina.

Some of the many people who have been influential on the course of the life of the author of this novel, and whom he has actually met - to some degree or another – in person are of the following names, titles, and descriptions:

(Spiritual) Grand Master Sheng-yen Lu

• (who, of course, would be Lu Sheng-yen in the Chinese convention in which surnames are first, rather than the English convention in which some form of the more-individually-oriented names are first) • (The author officially joined True Buddha School in October 2003 by taking refuge in GM Lu, yet, for the record, created this book completely outside of the auscpices of any officially sanctioned action from the scientifically and historically observable hierarchy of the human beings in that organization.) • (On a related note, the author draws inspiration and methods of effectiveness from many sources outside of the official instruction and training from any given source, even True Buddha School, yet similar to many other great leaders, Sheng-yen Lu in portions of his instructions encourages his sometimes-followers to use critical thinking, independent judgment, and zen transcendence over excessive leader-follower conceptualizations, whereas other parts of his instructions encourage sufficient regard for the value of leader-follower conceptualizations.)

(FIDE) Grand Master Garry Kasparov
(Although the author of this book first vividly became conscious of the legend of the chess extraordinaire Kasparov in 1993, up to the time of this publication the only meeting between the two occurred during a Garry Kasparov speech-and-book-signing event on January 27th, 2016 in connection with the book *Winter is Coming*.)

 Maurice A.T. Blair (1931-2015) (Father of this book's author, reflected by official family records of lineage)
   (The author is extremely thankful for his father's help with a multitude of developments in life, even with how the author has at times strongly disagreed on some topics and decisions. There have also been many cases of when the author has strongly agreed on topics and decisions.)
   (Thanks for a multitude or many myriads of multitudes of things, my father, and may you rest in peace in the situations in which you believe it appropriate. Or is this even an appropriate approach for me to take regarding you at all, given that one of the hypotheses that you, and others, have sometimes posited is the idea that the dead might go through eons of dreamless sleep before being awakened and summoned for judgment day?!)

Helga Sky Polega (either 1976-2002 or 1977-2002, as different online records at times support each notion of that[1]) • (A Duke University contemporary who started her freshman year when the author was starting his sophomore year) • (The author dated her twice, and he met her on a modest number of other occasions spread over several years. The author never reached base with her in terms of baseball metaphors for physical romance; perhaps related to this was how she mentioned on at least one occasion that she had made an agreement with her parents to refrain from getting seriously involved with anyone romantically during her undergraduate studies, hoping that this restriction would boost her chances for professional success. Most of the author's meetings with her were in the Fall Semester of 1995, a few were in 1996, and there was at least one occasion in 1997 and/or 1998. On another note, the author refrained from looking up her information on the Internet for many years, then wondered why she seemed absent from Facebook as of mid-2009. Upon then searching the Internet, he found out that she had died nearly eight years earlier.) • (Thanks for the memories, Sky, and please rest in peace if and when you can and should.)

David "Godot" Hoffman (a fellow Psi Upsilon Fraternity brother of the Chi Delta Chapter) (After the author turned down the fraternity's early-1995 offer for him to pledge, David Hoffman went out of his way to convince him to change his mind. The author indeed reconsidered, changed his mind, pledged the fraternity, and joined it.) (On another note, he graduated from Duke in 1997, yet I stated in a 2022 letter to him and several other people a reference to him as having graduated from that university in 1996. Records clearly show that he graduated form Duke University in 1997.)

Liza Darnton (the first woman whom the author truly dated, and who initiated the author into experiencing mouth-to-mouth kissing)

For the record, I have only knowingly met her in person in portions of the first half of 1995, neither she nor I made any overt attempt to go further than kissing each other in terms of physical romance between her and me.

The referenced date involved the Chi Delta Chapter of Psi Upsilon's Formal Dinner and Dance that happened in the evening and night of April 7th, 1995. After it became clear that she was going to go home with a female friend also in attendance at the event and with a person or multiple persons whom she and her friend met outside the auspices of the fraternity's gathering as part of stepping aside from the formal repeatedly, there arrived a moment of truth.

I expressed a strong preference for Liza to stay, yet she was clearly set on the path of leaving without me. Reality presented her with several options. She chose to hurry over to me, deliver fast-motion, repetitive kisses in a flash, then dash away. Her friend also left her date, another of the brothers, though in less dramatic fashion.

When Godot offered me a belated happy birthday wish on June 15, 2022 via Facebook, one day after the 6/14/2022 occurrence of my 46th birthday, this was the first domino in a chain reaction that fate had perfectly aligned: within days I felt best to carefully send a LinkedIn invitation to Liza. That led to her acceptance; Liza and I joined each other's networks on June 19, 2022 on LinkedIn.

Unbeknownst to Liza for a while, most likely from right after the 1995 date until I informed her about it via email on June 20th, 2022, I had been oriented by several of the fraternity brothers to view her set of decisions in a very negative light, and the mixture of goodwill and ill will that I had felt toward her had probably been one of the major contributors to some of the struggles I had with mental health and life in general as the years and decades had moved along, *until* when, in the twinkling of an eye, within about two seconds of when I found out that she had accepted my networking invitation on Father's Day 2022, I suddenly felt *total healing* from the previously conflicting orientations of ethos, logos, and pathos toward how to feel about what had transpired way back when.

The late wine enthusiast Barbara Hawkins, 1945-2013, who was my upstairs neighbor from mid-2002 to November 2005 and from early May 2006 to circa the end of September 2008, and who was my parents' upstairs neighbor from mid-2002 to circa the end of September 2008, should deserve credit for an assist with how Liza was able to grant me a profound long-term healing effect.[2,3,6,7]

Although I probably either never even mentioned to Barbara the very fact of existence of Liza or mentioned it fewer than three times, they both indicated to me, albeit at very different times and places, that they belong to the Greek organization known as Alpha Phi.

On one occasion in which I felt very down and out with life—a time which my memory indicates to have been approximately of the mid-May-to-mid-September 2003 period, Barbara Hawkins brought to me a sample of Alpha Phi Sorority jewelry, and she encouraged me to hold the jewelry for about a minute or two. I held that item or set of items—I do not remember for sure exactly how many there were, yet there was definitely at least one—for a while. As I held the jewelry, she spoke to me with kindness.

On another note, I estimate that it was not until about sometime 2010-2014 that I found out that Liza's father, John Darnton, is a prominent literary figure, and it was only after the 6/19/22 healing effect that I started to set out toward beginning to read his writings beyond available brief online previews of excerpts. I did speak with John Darnton by phone in an actual two-way conversation briefly one time on or about April 24 or 25, 2021. When he and I spoke with each other, it was a brief and reasonably friendly phone call, and neither of us made any specific requests from the other, yet we did briefly discuss Liza Darnton, Steven Spielberg, and other subjects. Please bear in mind that as of the time of publishing this book I have never met acclaimed director and film producer Steven Spielberg, yet I have seen over a dozen of the motion picture films that he has directed. Speaking with John Darnton on the phone in April 2021, whether anyone else on Earth thinks this was and/or is relevant to anything or not, caused me to become – as defined by some normal interpretations of reality – within two degrees of separation from that Director Spielberg, if not already unknowingly having reached two degrees of separation previously.

Oden Giffin (a man I met on September 10th, 2022 in Houston, TX, USA, and who expressed that he was a homeless person)

He said that people had stolen all of his identification cards sometime after he became homeless, and that he has been living continuously for a while in the absence of legal proof of identity in addition to his other difficulties.

His father, per his account, had intended for his legal name to have the spelling "Odin," yet, mysteriously, the U.S. government administrative people and/or computers somehow introduced a typographic variance by officially spelling it "Oden."

Before Dr. Dorsey Armstrong became the holder of a doctorate of philosophy and a Purdue University professor, she was a graduate student who met me in 1994 via a class for which she she served as the teacher. She was the University Writing Course instructor for a variety of students, including me, during my first semester at Duke University. For the record, the author of this book, up to the time of this publication, only met her in the Twentieth Century and neither dated nor partook of any romantic physical contact with her. There was at least one thorough hug, yet that was about caring as two human beings and not about romantic intent. I have had electronic mail correspondence with her on extremely rare occasions since finishing that Fall Semester 1994 course.[5,10])

Professor (and former professional boxer) William W. Cooper (1914-2012, and who was already a retired professor at The University of Texas at Austin as of a fateful day in the Spring Semester of 2002 when he made a special appearance to speak to the collected members of Dr. James Deitrick's class, which included me)

(Professional Boxer/Boxing Instructor) Jesus Poll (who guided some basic boxing training for the author during sessions from sometime in the second half of 2002 to early April 2003)

(Martial Arts Master/Instructor) Larry St. Clair (who provided basic Jeet Kune Do and Kali training to the author through a practical six-week-or-thereabouts self-defense course that happened in mid-2002)

Part III:

Also influential to the author of this novel, though in most regular senses "having never met" the author, and in some esoteric senses "having met at a distance" the author:

• Nobel Prize-Winning Artist Bob Dylan. He performed portions of a September 17, 1999 concert attended by many people, including my father and me, at a venue in The Woodlands, Texas. His co-headliner for the concert was Paul Simon. Bob Dylan music sometimes aired on the late radio station KKRW 93.7 FM (1993-2013, which, as per https://en.wikipedia.org/wiki/KQBT {as accessed 24 SEP 2024} ran from 25 NOV 1993 to midday 31 DEC 2013—just over twenty years & one month).

• Dame Olivia Newton-John (9/26/1948-8/8/2022). She delivered a 3/26/2010 speech and a 3/27/2010 concert in Pennsylvania that I attended in the absence of any of my close relatives—such as first cousins or closer—as far as I knew.

That being said, she did appear in some of my dreams on rare occasions after I found out in the second quarter of 2006 that she was the mystery singer of the popular recordings of "Let Me Be There" and "If You Love Me (Let Me Know)" which appeared on commercially-produced Asian-distribution mix tapes that I joyfully listened to many times during the prepubescent stage of this life. In 2003 I became reacquainted with those songs as they appeared on the late radio station Country Legends 97.1 FM (2003-2023, the Greater Houston, TX area, especially emanating from Cleveland, TX, eventually having its 97.1 FM registration bought out and then going away to be replaced at that frequency modulation setting for the Greater Houston area). For a while, I avoided looking up who the singer was out of a concern that learning the identity would add baggage to the songs, yet by sometime in 2Q 2006 I decided that the time would be right to finally discover who sang those two popular recordings that had super-resonated with me as a young child and which later super-resonated with me as an adult.

Those mix tapes had, for whatever reason(s) what I had long remembered as them having left a blank space where they could have otherwise named her, in contrast with how I had long remembered them to have named most of the artists on most of the tapes in their series. However, upon looking again at one of the tapes sometime circa 2023, I noticed that it actually left blank all the names of the performers of the recordings. Therefore, my memory of it having left her blank became more prominent to me, as in some of those earlier years I was able to determine the identities of some of the other artists and some of the bands without much difficulty, and it took decades for me to finally get around to knowing her to be the person with the voice that helped make those two John Rostill (1942-1973) songs into huge commercial successes. *Songs of Memory* was the series name for many of those music tapes that my household often played when I was very young.

Part IV

Although Yahoo! Groups went away years ago, I still vividly remember, among other things, having on December 25th, 2004 (as measured by Houston time) posted to the acc-list {which focused on the life and works of Arthur C. Clarke (1917-2008); its acronym stood either for "The Arthur C. Clarke List Yahoo! Group" or some very similar title} a link to the web page khandro.net, a web page emphasized much regarding the life and works of one of the claimants to the title of 17th Karmapa, and—in many respects—much more regarding a general survey of the vast arrays of interdisciplinary technologies and controversies from the Himalayas and everywhere else.[4]

Maurice James Blair
Houston, TX, USA
September 18, 21, 27, & 28, 2022; and September 20 & 24-26, 2024

ADDITIONAL GRAYSCALE GLIMPSES

••• This section provides extra context via a copy of a collection of photographs (presumably from the 20th century, in each case most likely with either Maurice A.T. Blair having served as the photographer or someone close to him having served as the photographer; among the photographs that the surviving members of my father's household inherited from him). Ming Y. Blair and Maurice J. Blair inherited the photographs from Maurice A.T. Blair. Maurice J. Blair and Synapsid Revelations Press are authorized to reprint here this set of glimpses from long ago.

ADDITIONAL GRAYSCALE GLIMPSES II

In this section are grayscale versions of glimpses of casual, intermediate-level, online, blitz chess action and black-and-white-and-gray glimpses of social media posting activity.

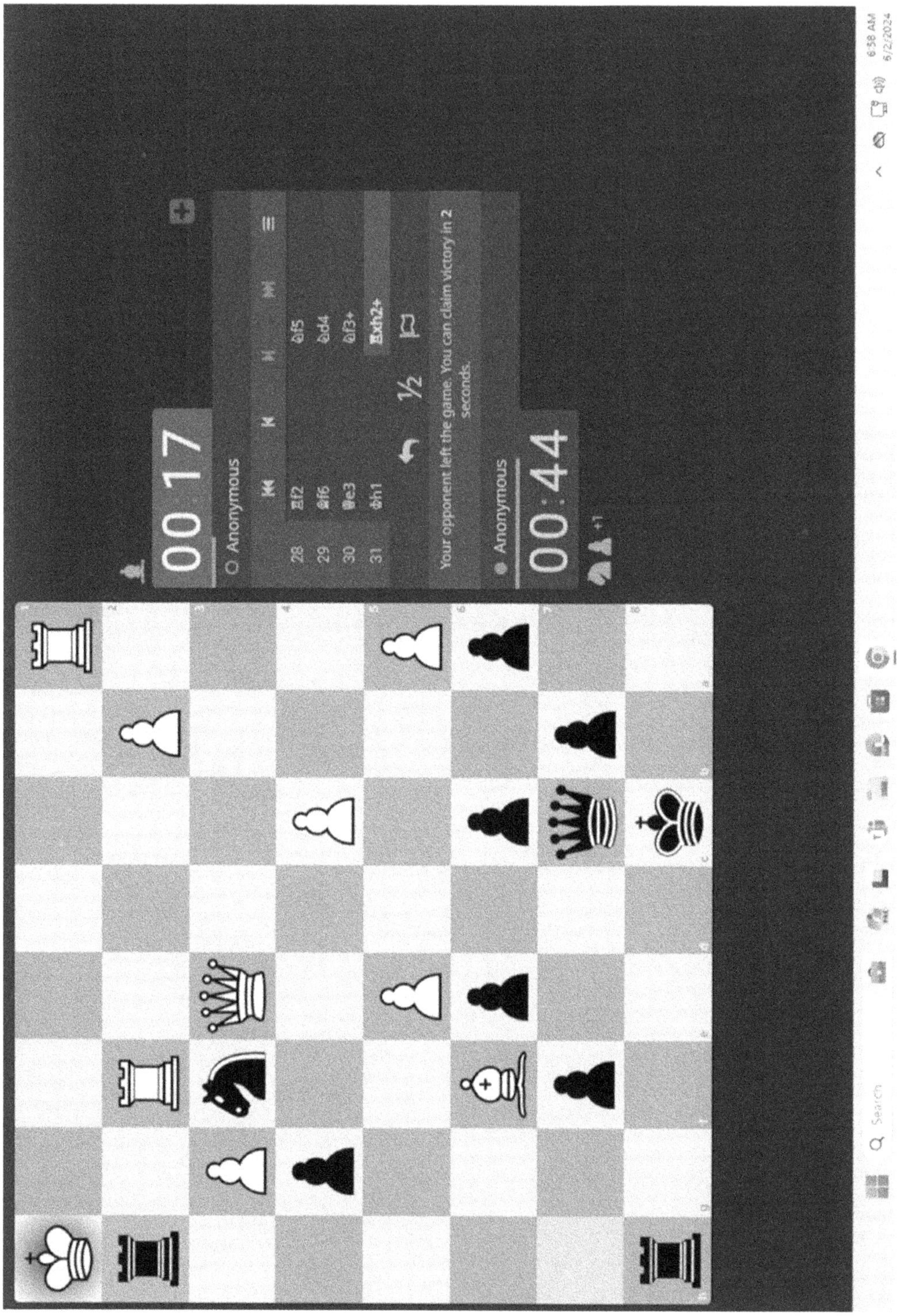
Anonymous
00:17
28 ♖f2 ♘f5
29 ♗f6 ♘d4
30 ♕e3 ♘f3+
31 ♔h1 ♖xh2+
½
Your opponent left the game. You can claim victory in 2 seconds.
Anonymous
00:44
+1
Search
6:58 AM
6/2/2024

lichess.org/axecXd2OxvkU
YouTube Maps
s.org PLAY PUZZLES LEARN WATCH COMMUNITY TOOLS
SIGN IN
05 56
Anonymous
2 c4 d5
3 cxd5 xd5
4 c3 c6
5 b5
½
Your opponent left the game. You can claim victory in 3 seconds.
Anonymous
02:00
3:10 PM
6/4/2024
·3 · Casual · Blitz
ght now
Search
Black + 15 seconds

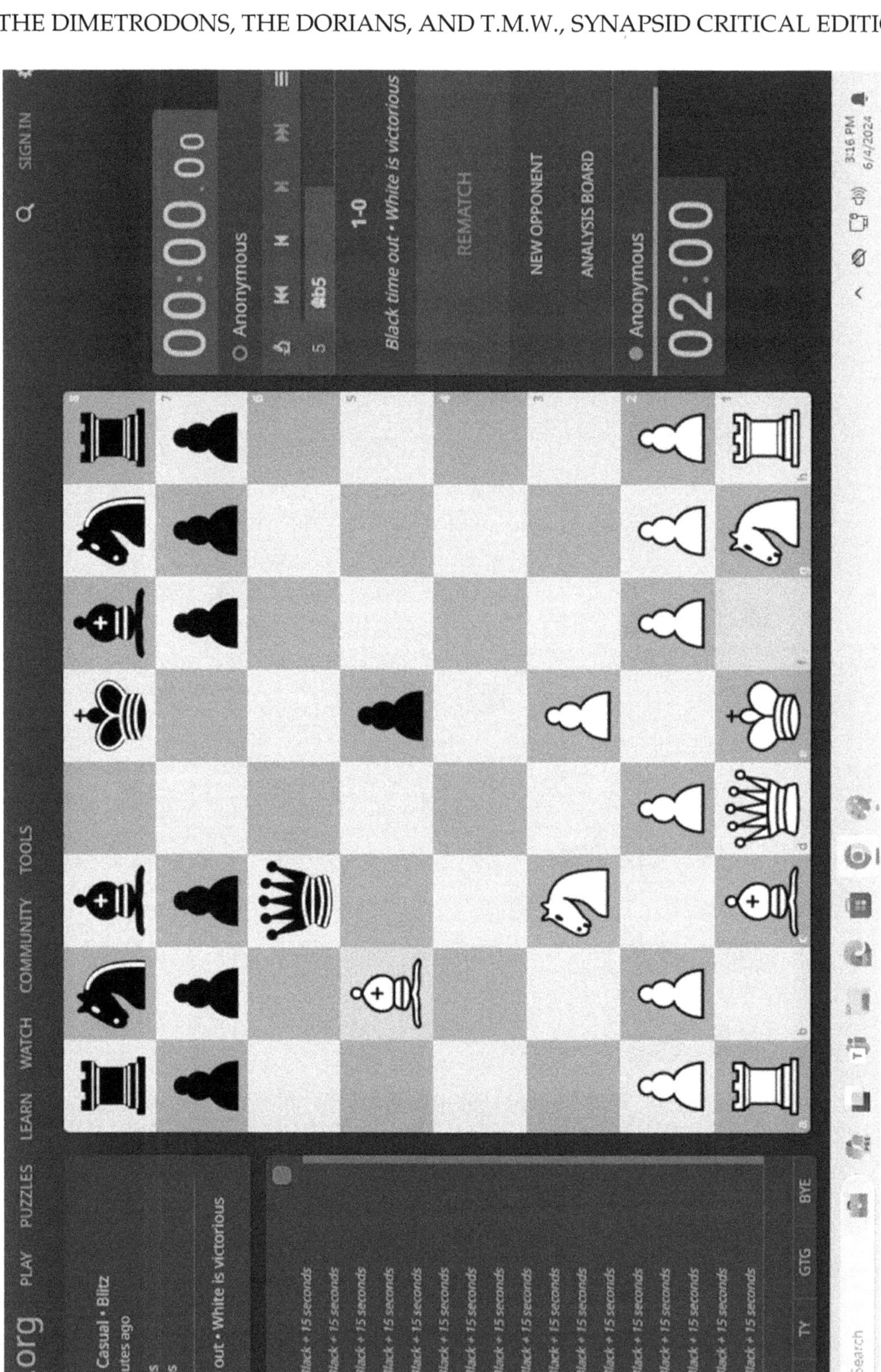

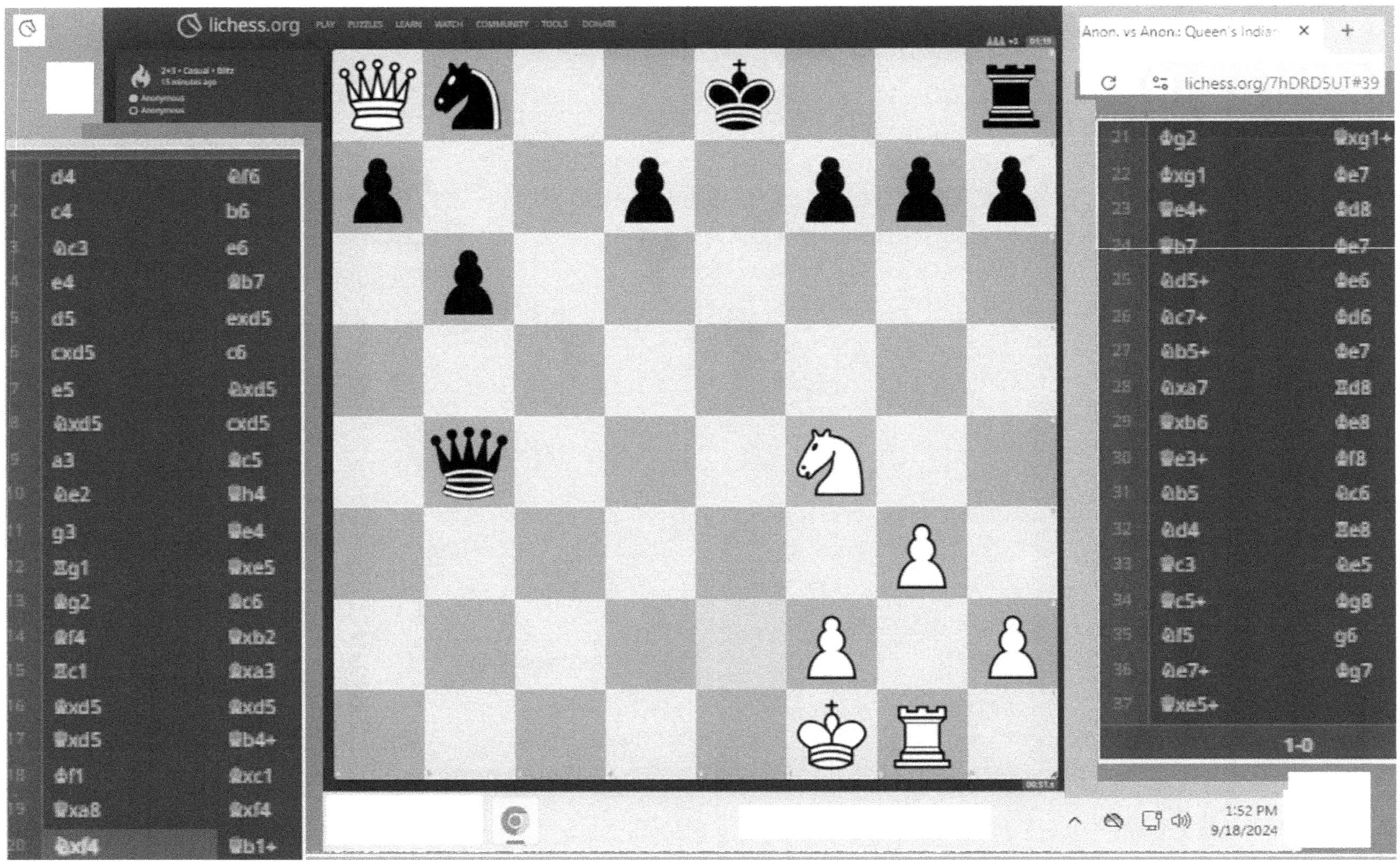

lichess.org   PLAY   PUZZLES   LEARN   WATCH   COMMUNITY   TOOLS   DONATE
Anon. vs Anon.: Queen's Indian
lichess.org/7hDRD5UT#39
2+3 • Casual • Blitz
15 minutes ago
Anonymous
Anonymous
1   d4   Nf6
2   c4   b6
3   Nc3   e6
4   e4   Bb7
5   d5   exd5
6   cxd5   c6
7   e5   Nxd5
8   Nxd5   cxd5
9   a3   Bc5
10 Ne2   Qh4
11 g3   Qe4
12 Rg1   Qxe5
13 Bg2   Qc6
14 Bf4   Qxb2
15 Rc1   Bxa3
16 Bxd5   Bxd5
17 Qxd5   Bb4+
18 Kf1   Bxc1
19 Qxa8   Bxf4
20 Qxf4   Qb1+
21 Kg2   Qxg1+
22 Kxg1   Ke7
23 Qe4+   Kd8
24 Qb7   Ke7
25 Nd5+   Ke6
26 Nc7+   Kd6
27 Nb5+   Ke7
28 Nxa7   Rd8
29 Qxb6   Ke8
30 Qe3+   Kf8
31 Nb5   Nc6
32 Nd4   Re8
33 Qc3   Ne5
34 Qc5+   Kg8
35 Nf5   g6
36 Ne7+   Kg7
37 Qxe5+
1-0
1:52 PM   9/18/2024

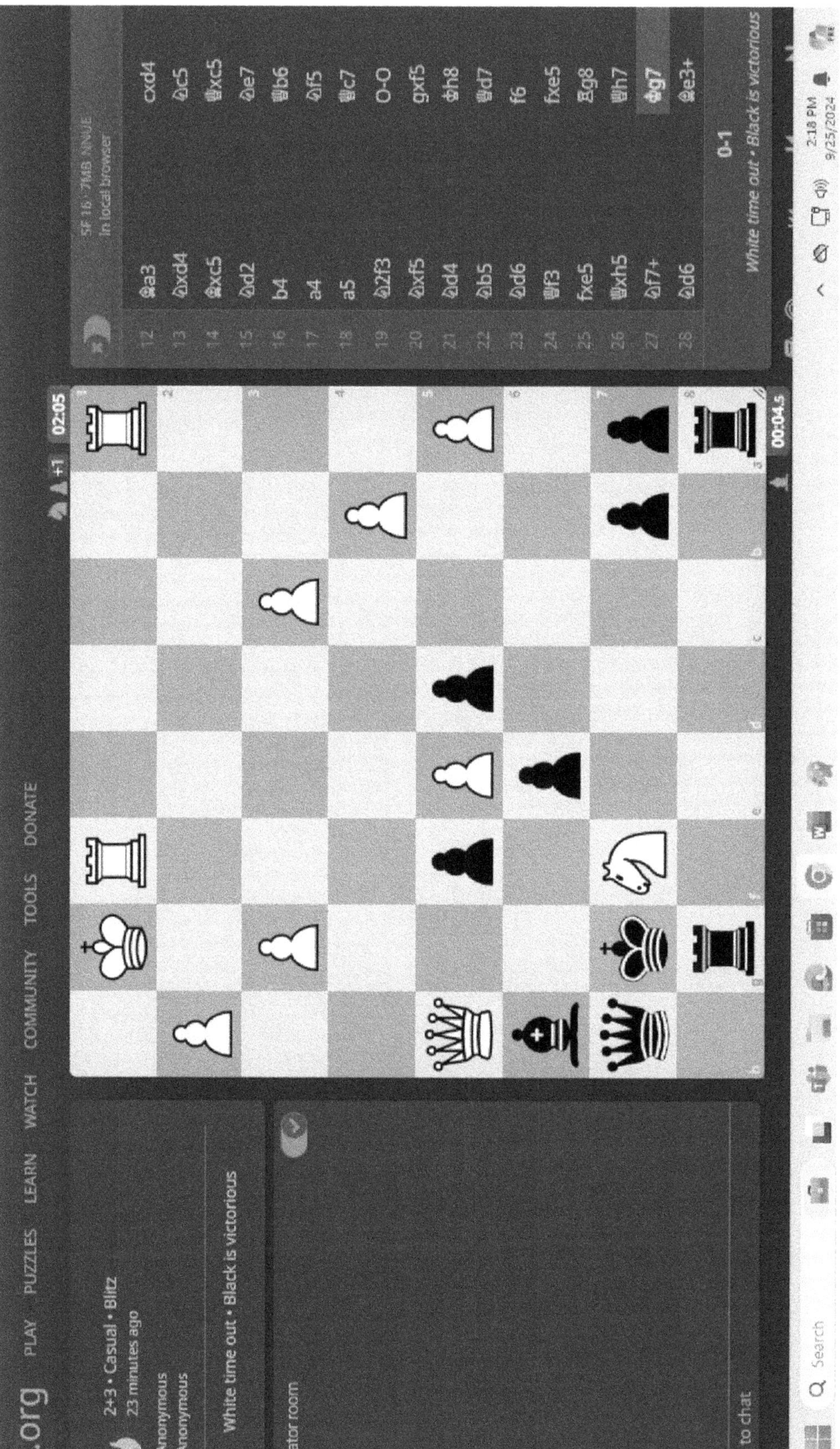
lichess.org/KEX5QopL/black#54
Maps
s.org   PLAY PUZZLES LEARN WATCH COMMUNITY TOOLS DONATE
2+3 • Casual • Blitz
23 minutes ago
Anonymous
Anonymous
White time out • Black is victorious
ctator room
in to chat
SF 16 · 7MB NNUE
In local browser
12 ♘a3   cxd4
13 ♘xd4   ♘c5
14 ♘xc5   ♕xc5
15 ♘d2   ♘e7
16 b4   ♕b6
17 a4   ♘f5
18 a5   ♕c7
19 ♘2f3   O-O
20 ♘xf5   gxf5
21 ♘d4   ♔h8
22 ♘b5   ♕d7
23 ♘d6   f6
24 ♕f3   fxe5
25 fxe5   ♖g8
26 ♕xh5   ♕h7
27 ♘f7+   ♔g7
28 ♘d6   ♘e3+
0-1
White time out • Black is victorious
2:18 PM
9/25/2024
Search
02:05
00:04.5

2+3 • Casual • Blitz
17 minutes ago
Anonymous
Anonymous
White time out • Black is victorious
spectator room
02:12
01:44
SF 16 - 7MB NNUE
in local browser
1 e4 c6
2 d4 d5
3 e5 Nf5
4 f4 h5
5 Nf3 g6
6 c3 e6
7 Nd3 Nxd3
8 Qxd3 Nh6
9 O-O Nd7
10 g3 Qb6
11 b3 c5
12 Ba3 cxd4
13 Nxd4 Nc5
14 Bxc5 Qxc5
15 Nd2 Ne7
16 b4 Qb6
17 a4 Nf5
18 a5 Qc7
19 N2f3 O-O
20 Nxf5 gxf5
21 Nd4 Kh8
22 Nb5 Qd7
23 Nd6 f6
24 Qf3 fxe5
25 fxe5 Rg8
26 Qxh5 Qh7
27 Nf7+ Kg7
28 Nd6 Be3+
0-1
White time out • Black is victorious
search
2:11 PM
9/25/2024

Here is a September 26, 2024 edited and expanded variation:

Although some model communication styles as assertive, passive, aggressive, and passive-aggressive, that model skips omnicritical (as in Bob Dylan's song "Idiot Wind") and cloak-and-dagger (as in the trilogy *House of Cards* (1990), *To Play the King* (1993), and *The Final Cut* (1995)).

A more complete model might consist of the set of those six styles and the all-accomplishing style (as in transcending each style by correctly matching styles to instances of reality, much as some believe Jeet Kune Do, Kabbalist Judaism, Kabbalist Noahidism, Esoteric Christianity, Sufi Islam, Esoteric People-of-the-Book-ism, Zen Buddhism, and Vajrayana Buddhism to encourage beings to strive toward achieving).

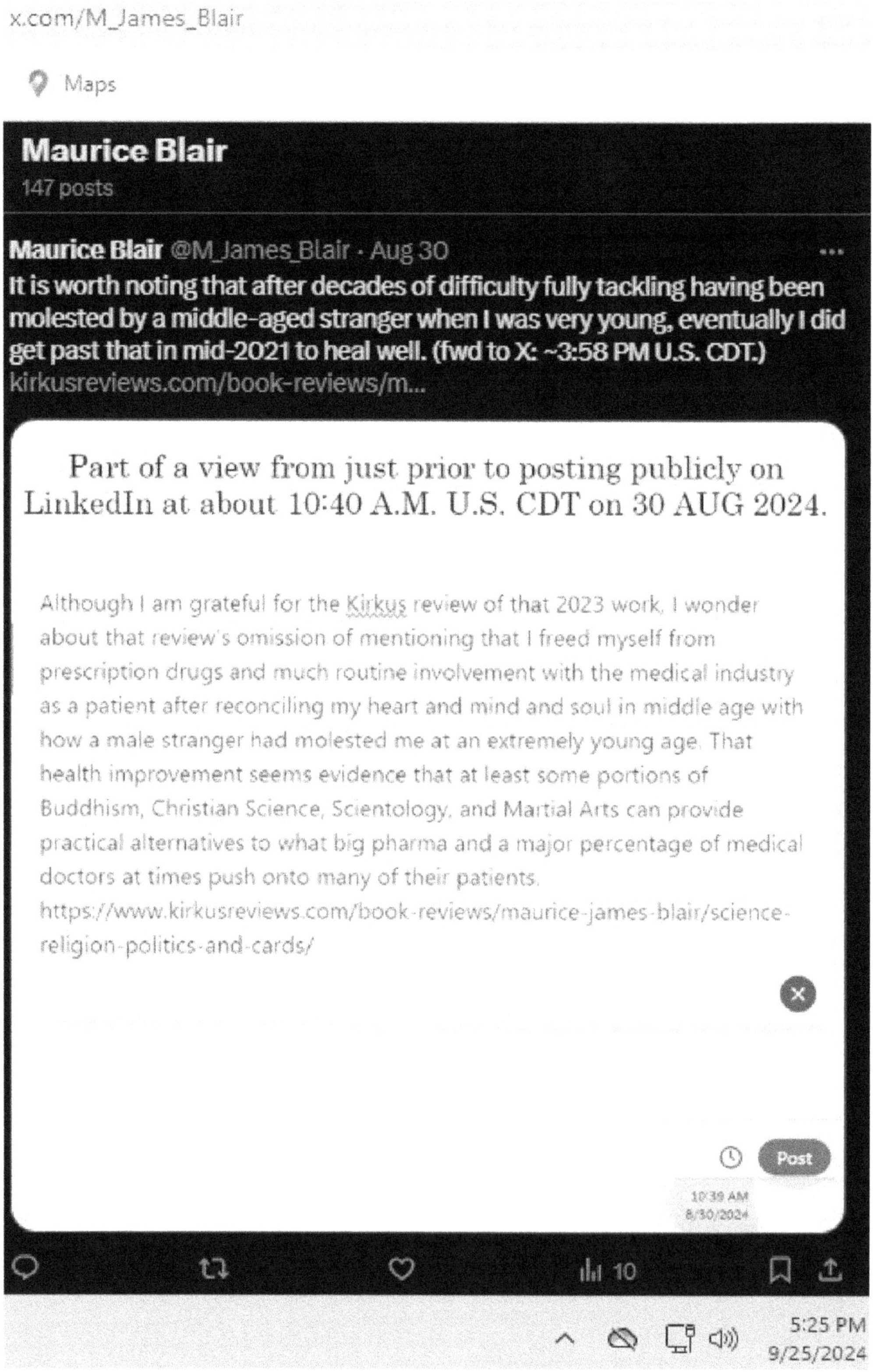

x.com/M_James_Blair

 Maps

Maurice Blair
147 posts

Maurice Blair @M_James_Blair · Aug 30
It is worth noting that after decades of difficulty fully tackling having been molested by a middle-aged stranger when I was very young, eventually I did get past that in mid-2021 to heal well. (fwd to X: ~3:58 PM U.S. CDT.)
kirkusreviews.com/book-reviews/m...

Part of a view from just prior to posting publicly on LinkedIn at about 10:40 A.M. U.S. CDT on 30 AUG 2024.

Although I am grateful for the Kirkus review of that 2023 work, I wonder about that review's omission of mentioning that I freed myself from prescription drugs and much routine involvement with the medical industry as a patient after reconciling my heart and mind and soul in middle age with how a male stranger had molested me at an extremely young age. That health improvement seems evidence that at least some portions of Buddhism, Christian Science, Scientology, and Martial Arts can provide practical alternatives to what big pharma and a major percentage of medical doctors at times push onto many of their patients.
https://www.kirkusreviews.com/book-reviews/maurice-james-blair/science-religion-politics-and-cards/

Post

10:39 AM
8/30/2024

10

5:25 PM
9/25/2024

A CHART OF SOME DIFFERENCES BETWEEN VARIATIONS

A SAMPLE OF DIFFERENCES BETWEEN T.D.T.D.A.T.M.W. 1st & 2nd PRINTINGS, T.D.T.D.A.T.M.W.:R.E., and T.D.T.D.A.T.M.W.S.C.E.

Crit.Ed. p.#	1st Pr. TDTDATM (with 8.5" x 11" pages)	2nd Pr. TDTDATM (with 8.5" x 11" pages)	TDTDATM:Rev. Ed. (with 5.5" x 8.5" pages)	T.D.T.D.A.T.M.W.: Critical Edition (with 8.5" x 11" pages)
16	p. 13: "274,578 years"	p. 13: "274,578 millennia"	p. 19 "274,578,000 years"	p. 16 "274,578 millennia"
72	p. 66: "prinordial"	p. 66: "prinordial"	p. 82 "primordial"	p. 72 "primordial"
N/A	p. 85: "pation"	p. 85: "patient"	N/A: (omitted)	N/A: (omitted)
94	p. 87: "c.1976-2001"	p. 87: "c.1976-2001"	N/A: (omitted)	p. 94 "either 1977-2002 or 1976-2002, as different online records at times support each notion of that"

ENDNOTES:

[1] For that Sky Polega, here is a survey of online differences of what some URLs indicate for the chronology of her birth and her death:

The site ancientfaces.com/person/Helga-s-polega-birth-1976-death-2002/32178503 (as accessed on August 14, 2024 and September 20, 2024) indicated that she was born on December 8, 1976 and that she died on September 7, 2002.

In contrast with that, the site https://sbags.org/immigrant/d0058/I55241.html (as accessed on July 6, 2024) indicated that she was born on an unspecified date in 1977 and that she died on September 8, 2002.

Here is a zoomed-in portion of a November 3, 1995 Chi Delta Chapter of Psi Upsilon Semiformal dinner and dance event photograph. In this, Sky is on the viewer's right, and I am on the viewer's left.

The author and the publisher are uncertain who served as the photographer, yet both the publisher and the author assert that having a modified-into-grayscale-and-cropped-as-part-of-context manifestation of that photograph is well within the legal rights. After the semiformal, the author received a personal copy of the source photograph, which included additional people.

[2] Consider two photographs from circa December 2002 at a gathering at what was then Barbara Hawkins' apartment unit, adjusted to grayscale, one on this page, and another on the next page:

From left to right: Maurice A.T. Blair, Ming Y. Blair, and Barbara Hawkins.

To the best of my knowledge, I, Maurice James Blair, served as the photographer for the above photo. I scanned it from a physical, full-color photograph.

From left to right: Maurice James Blair, Ming Y. Blair, and Barbara Hawkins.

Maurice A.T. Blair was almost definitely the photographer for that one.

I, Maurice James Blair, scanned it into grayscale from a full-color polaroid-style picture, then slightly cropped it before arranging for it to appear here.

---

[3] Cf. *Science, Religion, Politics, and Cards* (2023), *Alternative Beginnings and Endings of All Things: Science, Religion, Politics, and Cards, Hypervolume II* (2024), and *Simplicity, Intricacy, and Beyond: Science, Religion, Politics, and Cards, Hypervolume III* (2024).

---

[4] The claimant His Holiness Urgyen Trinley Dorje is the 17th Karmapa who uses khandro.net as his website, whereas, in contrast, the claimant His Holiness Thaye Dorje is the 17th Karmapa who uses karmapa.org as his website.[10] Reference: Those pages as accessed on September 20, 2024 and on some previous occasions.

[5] Next, consider a copy of one of the revised papers from that UWC course, and it includes references to the Sgt. Ronald Turner[6] also known as Mr. Turner, who taught a course that I attended during my senior year of high school:

Jim Blair

Armstrong-UWC 5

Portfolio - Assignment 3B

Better Education

A few months ago, if someone had asked me, "What single thing can our society do to improve the well-being of all future generations?" I would have been dumbfounded. My mind would have splintered into a dozen different directions and gone round and round, and I wouldn't be able to make a coherent answer. Now, however, I have something to say about the matter. Improving the education children receive at home and at school is paramount to social progress.

"Improving the education children receive at home and at school is paramount to social progress" is a vague statement. It can be understood to mean any one of a million different things, but I firmly support it, interpreting it as follows: "If we can better foster free-thinking and open-mindedness to the possibility that one's own opinions could be wrong, and raise the overall level of education, then immeasurable social progress will ensue." An experience I had this past summer led me to this conclusion.

It happened while I was working at "Call 'n China", a carryout-and-delivery Chinese food place. One night a delivery driver and I were sitting behind the counter and talking because business was slow. He was a white, thirty-eight-year-old high school dropout. Also, I had learned from numerous conversations with him that his parents were extremely strict: they trained him to do *and* think as he was told. A group of black teens walked by outside and he said, "You see those kids? They've been stealing cokes from us. But I caught 'em the other day, so they won't mess with us when they see me. They steal from us as a test. If they think it's easy to steal, someday they'll come in with a gun and

rob us."

He seemed a little paranoid to me. I asked, "What if one of them came in here to

order something and he really was an honest customer?"

He answered, "You have to judge whether people are going to be good customers

or if they're just trying to take advantage of us."

I retorted, "So should I keep a close watch on all customers?"

"No," he replied. "You have to watch certain people more carefully. You have to

watch kids carefully. If someone is...[he seemed to struggle for a word] respectable, then

you don't have to watch 'em so close." This statement took me aback. There seemed to

be some kind of racial innuendo in the way he said it and the look he gave me. A

statement of "can't you see what I'm saying about blacks" seemed to emanate from his

stare.

Several more incidents followed. One day he explained that he thought America

was going to hell, and blacks were to blame for it; on another occasion he vehemently

griped that blacks didn't tip him very well; another time he came back from a delivery and

said that the blacks he delivered to paid him out of a big stack of money, and they

therefore must have been drug-dealers.

Every time he said one of these things I argued with him, trying to explain to him

why the things he said were not necessarily true. I could never get anywhere with arguing

with him, though, because he could only argue with emotion. His poor education had

given him an inability to use logic and reason to consider other people's ideas. He could

only see argument in terms of "I am right and you are wrong."

It would be ridiculous to jump to the conclusion that people with more education

are necessarily better than people with less education. Many poorly-educated people do

great things, and many well-educated people do very wicked things; this may be

attributable to their values and whether they follow their conscience. By "values," I mean the ideas they have been taught by parents, teachers, friends, and others. For example, someone might be taught that racial differences are superficial and do not, in and of themselves, make a person better or worse. Someone else might be taught that blacks are subhuman. If they are both trained to believe in these values and never question them or consider alternatives, then they are equally indoctrinated and narrow-minded. It just happens that the former person was imparted with a good value and the latter with a bad one. "Well-educated" people are often just as narrow-minded as "poorly-educated people" if we take the quantity of education (i.e., the number of years of schooling or highest grade-level reached) to be the same as the quality of education.

But the key point that can be learned from my experience is that either a poor education or being trained to think narrow-mindedly can severely hinder moral and intellectual growth, enslaving one to the attitudes and beliefs that one is told to uphold, or whatever attitudes and beliefs are most emotionally appealing. A good education can provide freedom from this. By good education, I mean being taught to keep an open mind. One might say that the very act of teaching someone to think openly is a form of indoctrination, and, in a strict linguistic sense, (s)he would be right. Teaching anyone anything might be considered indoctrination, but training one to question one's beliefs is a special kind of indoctrination: it permits one to even question *whether questioning* one's beliefs is right or wrong. Anyone sensible who is given this training will decide that it is both in his/her best interest and the best interest of society that (s)he think openly, because it is only by examining all possible views that one can hope to find the truth in any matter. In this way, the fact that teaching someone to think openly is a form of indoctrination in the strict linguistic sense is trivial; teaching someone to think openly frees that person from any form of indoctrination, including the idea that (s)he should think with an open mind. Higher levels of education tend to encourage open-mindedness more than lower levels of education, although this is not always reliable because the quality of an education depends greatly on the quality of each individual instructor.

I recall a scene from my US Government class in high school. The teacher, Mr.

Turner, had just taught the basic idea of Hobbes's social contract theory:
> "Ancient man--caveman, let's say--created governments by agreement.
> With complete freedom and no control, life was nasty, brutish, and short.
> Consequently, cavemen came together and agreed to follow the authority
> of one caveman. In doing so, they lost much of their freedom, but gained
> law and order. Life was improved greatly."

Then he turned to the class and asked, "How many of you agree with Hobbes's theory?"

Most of us raised our hands to agree.

> Next he countered with another theory on the formation of government:
> "One caveman was stronger, bigger, and badder than the other cavemen.
> He used brute force to gain authority over the others."

Mr. Turner asked us, "Now, how many of you agree with this biggest, baddest caveman

theory?"

Once again, most of us raised our hands. He explained to us that we shouldn't

simply accept ideas we hear as being true because they *seem* to be well-supported. We

should start with a skeptical view of any idea, examine alternatives and different aspects of

the subject, and then form conclusions. Even then, he said, we should remain open-

minded to other possibilities.

People who have been taught to think openly, and not to assume anyone's ideas on

anything to be true, have the potential to improve themselves, to adopt new views and

attitudes when they find their present ones lacking. People who are undereducated and

trained to think as they are told, will reject anything that contradicts the attitudes and

beliefs they have adopted over time. If our society can challenge more children to view

issues from multiple perspectives, re-evaluate their own attitudes and beliefs frequently,

and think openly, we will have greatly ameliorated all social problems.

[6] Here are a few additional highlights I witnessed of what the J.M Hanks High School instructor Ronald Turner (who was usually known to his students as Mr. Turner) presented:

• On one occasion approximately April 1994 plus or minus a month or two, he said a joke to the students present, with words to this effect:

A Republican and a Democrat are sitting at a bar. The Democrat says to the Republican, "How are your efforts going?"

The Republican says, "We have been working hard to get out the vote. We don't know if it will be enough, but we've been working hard at it. How are your efforts going?"

The Democrat smiles, then says, "Don't you know? We Democrats know how to get the dead to turn out and vote for us!"

• He contemplated a report that Prince Charles showed clear signs of being totally unperturbed immediately after David Kang fired blank shots at him in protest in January 1994, then announced that anyone who truly and immediately bought into such a report alleging that royal calmness under pressure would have to be an Anglophile.

• He was the high school U.S. government teacher mentioned without being directly named on page 23 of *Alternative Beginnings and Endings of All Things*.[9,10]

• On one occasion in class he accidentally referred to King James I of England as having been the fourth of Scottish kings to have the King James name pattern, and I politely corrected him in class, mentioning how he had been the sixth of the Scottish kings to have the King James name pattern. He looked it up in an official record, then admitted to the class that I had been right to correct him.[10]

• I was among the students who chose, out of multiple options, to study *The Federalist Papers* (Hamilton, Madison, and Jay, 1788) and take an exam on them. I got almost everything correct on the exam, yet he pointed out to me that I missed the most important multiple question, the correct answer to which should have formed a statement—whether with these words or phrasing very similar—to the effect that, "Too much power concentrated in too few groups can be a grievous threat to liberty."[10]

• Although he characterized himself as a bleeding-heart liberal, he expressed strong support for the Second Amendment's protection of gun-ownership rights.[10]

• On at least one occasion, while many students were seated and waiting for the regular part of class to officially begin, he played a Johnny Cash (1932-2003) recording of the song "Daddy Sang Bass" {written by Carl Perkins (1932-1998)}.

[7] I have noticed competing influences—much of the online presence of Liza Darnton's family seems to lean much toward liberal politics, my late father leaned very much toward conservative politics in most ways, Ronald Turner was a liberal when he presented lectures in 1994, Anthony Holubik II has presented on multiple occasions in 2022 and 2024 being a conservative, Sean Hannity is conservative, LeBron James is liberal, Dana White is conservative, and so on and so forth.[10]

Suddenly, while composing this endnote, I had a flashback to sometime in the 2000-2002 period in Austin when Afolabi Ojumu (also known by his nickname, Fola), who was then attending the McCombs School of Business, was in a conversation with several other students. Each of several students would say something about who the student would be planning to vote for, who the student voted for, or both in some U.S. political context. When it arrived to be Fola's turn he said, either word-for-word or nearly word-for-word, "I'll exercise my right to the secret ballot in this case."

Perhaps more interesting is to compare and contrast (a) how Afolabi Ojumu sometime circa mid-2002 said to me that if enough people around one person rig a situation to make it impossible for that individual to win, then that individual will not be able to win, because of how much the others simply refuse to let that individual win and (b) how Olivia Newton-John in the song "Why Me" encouraged listeners to never give up on the hope that as long as they would be conscious there might be a chance to turn their situation around for the better, repeatedly emphasizing the phrase "Why Not Me" within that song.[8]

[8] *Gaia: One Woman's Journey* (1994).

[9] There were several differences between the promotional paperback (with text lightly revised 5/23/2024 from the initial 5/21/2024 transmission setup of it) and the regular-distribution hardcover (with text lightly revised 5/23/2024-5/24/2024) of *Alternative Beginnings and Endings of All Things*. Consider the document copied such as to appear on the next page.

A June 5, 2024 Memo Planned for Later Inclusion (with or without subsequent editing) in *The Dimetrodons, the Dorians, and the Modern World, Synapsid Critical Edition*

Alternate Title: A Memorandum Regarding Some Changes From the Rev. Date 5/23/2024 Text (with the promo. pbk) and the Rev. Date 5/24/2024 Text (with the reg. distr. h.c.) of *Alternative Beginnings and Endings of All Things:*

- There were adjustments to the copyright page.
- A few typos became fixed; for example, an occurrence of "psychologyical" adjusted into one of the many occurrences of "psychological."
- A few of the instances that would have gone with 381 years lower than the largest year number of the T.C. set of three had shown with a number 380 years lower, and the May Twenty Fourth revision adjusted these into having the 381 difference setting.
- A few of the instances of the version of The Tibetan Year 1,153 years lower than the largest year number of the set of three had shown with a number 1,152 years lower; the 5/24 revision adjusted these into having the 1,153 difference setting.
- The p. 378 reference to FEB 2024 changed into a p. 378 reference to FEB 2022.
- With the 380 vs. 381, with the 1,152 vs. 1,153, and with the FEB 2022 vs. FEB 2024, both the 5/23 version and the 5/24 version can be true, yet the 5/24 version for each of these three is more straight forwardly truthful. (Note 1: There can be unlimited alternative settings for where to place a Year 1 marker.) (Note 2: Mindsets in FEB 2024 included some recurrence of FEB 2022 mindsets.)
- Three of the e mail addresses became redacted.
- Adding a pp.580 613 set of references to #21 #28.

Another June 5, 2024 Memo Planned for Later Inclusion (with or without subsequent editing) in *The Dimetrodons, the Dorians, and the Modern World, Synapsid Critical Edition*

Alternate Title:
A Memorandum Regarding Some Unusual Features that Stayed the Same in the Rev. Date 5/24/2024 Text After Having Appeared in the Rev. Date 5/23/2024 Text

- Referring to *The Tonight Show Starring Johnny Carson* as "*The Tonight Show Starring Johnny Carson Show*" on page 377.

- Referring to Reba McEntire as "Reba McEntyre" on page 693.

- Referring to Jon Redmond as "John Redmond" on page 313.

- The title of the Mary Chapin Carpenter song "Where Time Stands Still" appears on p. 609 as "The Place Where Time Stands Still."

Revisit now portions of the September 3, 2019 Search that appeared in the preface:

"dorian and mycenaen teamwork"

Q All   Images   ▶ Videos   News

Your search - **"dorian and mycenaen teamwork"** - did not match any documents.

Suggestions:

- Make sure all words are spelled correctly.
- Try different keywords.
- Try more general keywords.

9/3/2019

Google

"dorian and mycenaen teamwork" - Google Search

Q

Shopping   More   Settings   Tools

77063, Houston, TX - From your device - Use precise location - Learn more

Help   Send feedback   Privacy   Terms

/search?ei=ue5uXdjqDln0tAXO9q_gAg&q="dorian+and+mycenaen+teamwork"&oq="dorian+and+mycenaen+teamwork"&gs_l...

1/1

[10] I mentioned on page 515 of *Alternative Beginnings and Endings of All Things: Science, Religion, Politics, and Cards, Hypervolume II* a reference to up to the time of the May 2024 publication of that book not yet having watched the *Star Trek: The Next Generation* episode "Justice" (1987). Subsequently, I did get around to watching that episode on June 8, 2024 from about 6:30 to about 7:48 A.M. Central Daylight Time in Houston, TX, USA. If you have not yet witnessed that episode, then please consider sooner or later witnessing it. If you have watched it, then consider reflecting on it.

Similarly, please bear in mind the presence of the audiovisual cultural artifacts in our reality listed here next to one bullet point each:

- *The 39 Steps* (1935)

- "TV or Not TV" (1955) / *The Honeymooners*

- "Judgment Night" (1959) / *The Twilight Zone*

- *The Way of the Dragon* (1972)

- *Pat Garrett and Billy the Kid* (1973)

- *Westminster: Behind Closed Doors* (1995)

- *Seven Years in Tibet* (1997)

- *Titanic* (1997)

- *Everest* (1998)

- *Magnolia* (1999)

- *Hotel Rwanda* (2004)

- *300* (2007)

- *Australia* (2008)

- *Thor: The Dark World* (2013)

- *300: Rise of an Empire* (2014)

- *Transformers: The Last Knight* (2017)

- "You Might Also Like" (2020) / *The Twilight Zone*

- *Ant-Man and the Wasp: Quantumania* (2023)

- *Transformers One* (2024)

Consider this: However real or unreal anyone else might seem to you, anyone else can contemplate however real or unreal you might seem to them.